Y0-CDF-258

"Don't you think it's time we stopped fighting?"

The quiet, low voice stopped Tamsin in her tracks. Jordan Keston in the role of peacemaker?

"Four years is a long time to hold a grudge. Don't you think it's time to forgive me?"

The dark-lashed blue eyes were beginning to mesmerize her, make her feel disoriented. She tried to break his gaze but seemed powerless to do so. "Forgive you?" she repeated huskily.

"For rejecting you. For not taking a frustrated nineteen-year-old virgin to my bed...."

Rosemary Gibson was born in Egypt. She spent the
early part of her childhood in Greece and Vietnam, and
now lives in the New Forest. She has had numerous
jobs, ranging from working with handicapped children,
collecting litter, being a gas station attendant to airline
ground hostess, but she has always wanted to be a
writer. She was lucky enough to have her first short
story accepted some years ago and now writes full-time.
She enjoys swimming, playing hockey, gardening
and traveling.

Books by Rosemary Gibson

HARLEQUIN ROMANCE
3344—NO TIES

HARLEQUIN PRESENTS
1403—TO TRUST A STRANGER
1474—AN UNEQUAL PARTNERSHIP

Don't miss any of our special offers. Write to us at the
following address for information on our newest releases.

Harlequin Reader Service
U.S.: 3010 Walden Ave., P.O. Box 1325, Buffalo, NY 14269
Canadian: P.O. Box 609, Fort Erie, Ont. L2A 5X3

The Bride's Daughter
Rosemary Gibson

Harlequin Books

TORONTO • NEW YORK • LONDON
AMSTERDAM • PARIS • SYDNEY • HAMBURG
STOCKHOLM • ATHENS • TOKYO • MILAN
MADRID • WARSAW • BUDAPEST • AUCKLAND

If you purchased this book without a cover you should be aware
that this book is stolen property. It was reported as "unsold and
destroyed" to the publisher, and neither the author nor the
publisher has received any payment for this "stripped book."

ISBN 0-373-03414-8

THE BRIDE'S DAUGHTER

First North American Publication 1996.

Copyright © 1996 by Rosemary Gibson.

All rights reserved. Except for use in any review, the reproduction or
utilization of this work in whole or in part in any form by any electronic,
mechanical or other means, now known or hereafter invented, including
xerography, photocopying and recording, or in any information storage
or retrieval system, is forbidden without the written permission of the
publisher, Harlequin Enterprises Limited, 225 Duncan Mill Road,
Don Mills, Ontario, Canada M3B 3K9.

All characters in this book have no existence outside the imagination of
the author and have no relation whatsoever to anyone bearing the same
name or names. They are not even distantly inspired by any individual
known or unknown to the author, and all incidents are pure invention.

This edition published by arrangement with Harlequin Books S.A.

® and TM are trademarks of the publisher. Trademarks indicated with
® are registered in the United States Patent and Trademark Office, the
Canadian Trade Marks Office and in other countries.

Printed in U.S.A.

CHAPTER ONE

'I DON'T believe it! He's thinking of coming to the wedding!'

'Your father's thinking of flying all the way from Sydney? To attend your mother's wedding to another man?' The fair-headed young man shot a quick glance at the slim girl who sat beside him in the passenger seat as he drove competently along the busy dual carriageway. 'That's a little unusual,' he added cautiously.

'But typical of my parents!' Tamsin Reed said wryly, stowing the airmail letter she'd just read back in her handbag. Hazel eyes beneath their sweep of thick, dark lashes gazed bleakly at the passing countryside bathed in the early-morning spring sunshine. Long, silky brown hair framed her oval face, emphasized the high cheekbones and wide, generous mouth set above a small, unexpectedly determined chin. 'I mean, why can't they be normal and fight and argue like most divorced couples?' Her mouth curved in a grin, but the flippancy in her voice was at war with the unhappiness in her eyes. 'I just don't understand any of it. They still care about each other, like each other. I always thought...' She furrowed her forehead. 'In fact, if it wasn't for that damn man I'm sure they would have got back together,' she muttered vehemently.

'I thought you liked Andrew. Isn't it the next exit?'

Tamsin bent her head to consult the map, the sweep of soft hair cascading over her shoulder, shielding her

5

face. 'Mmm. Then first left after the roundabout.' She wriggled her feet back into the navy blue court shoes she'd discarded earlier. 'I do like Andrew,' she admitted with reluctant but innate honesty, thinking briefly of the courteous, unassuming widower who would shortly be her stepfather. 'It's not him. It's his son.' Her husky voice and golden, green-flecked eyes reflected her contempt. 'Junior,' she added derogatorily. 'If he hadn't interfered, practically forced them together...he's the most manipulative, conniving...' She pressed her lips together, swallowing back a lurid epithet.

That was one of the drawbacks of sharing a house with three rugby-playing males, she thought with rueful amusement. It was all too easy to pick up some of their less admirable habits. Not that she would be sharing with them for much longer, she reminded herself with a pang of sadness. She was going to miss them.

Her eyes flicked to the favourite of her flatmates. Especially Tom, she mused wistfully, and his undemanding, uncomplicated friendship. It was he who had helped her through the bewilderment and misery of her parents' long separation and ensuing divorce.

Deliberately, she pushed the painful memories to the back of her mind, her expressive eyes lighting up with curiosity and interest as she caught her first glimpse of their destination.

'Bit of a contrast to Gatwick,' Tom echoed her first thought as he reduced speed and turned into the entrance of the south-coast airport, which until now had just been a name on a map. Glancing to the left, she surveyed the small, one-storey building, which was opposite a field of grazing cattle. One extreme to the other, she thought, fighting back the sudden inane desire to burst into giggles. How on earth would she ever adjust to this after the frenzied activity of the major airport?

'Still, you don't have to take the job even if you're offered it.' Tom turned into the staff car park as instructed in the letter inviting her for the interview.

Tamsin shrugged noncommittally. The interview was a mere formality, with her going through the motions for appearance sake. Little more than a casual chat to discuss pay and conditions. She'd been given a verbal assurance that the post of senior duty officer was hers. And Tom was wrong. She did have to take the job. Unemployed for the past five months since the airline for which she'd worked had gone into receivership, she was in no position to do anything else. In no position to tell her loathed benefactor exactly what he could do with his job offer, had instead been forced to swallow her pride, fight her every instinct and accept.

'Thanks for bringing me down,' she said, smiling, as Tom pulled to a halt. Dwindling savings had forced her to sell her own car a month ago. Fishing in her handbag, she retrieved a comb, ran it through her silky curtain of hair and wound it with practised skill into a neat chignon at the base of her neck. Checking her face in a small compact mirror, she reapplied pink gloss to her lips and, reaching in the back of the car for her jacket, slipped it over her crisp cream blouse.

'How do I look?' She grinned at her companion. 'Efficient? Capable? Business-like?' She was completely unaware that the overriding impression was one of total femininity, that the subtle hint of slender curves beneath the utilitarian blue suit was far more tantalizing than any blatant emphasis, that the severe hairstyle drew instant attention to the lovely, dark fringed eyes.

'You look ... wow!'

'Now don't overdo it,' she murmured drily, her gaze immediately following Tom's as it rested admiringly on the sleek, silver grey sports car that slid into a space at the far end of the car park.

'Isn't that—?'

'Yes,' she cut in, her expression tightening. 'The man himself. Jordan Keston.'

Jordan Keston. The legendary troubleshooter who invested in ailing companies and turned them into viable commercial concerns. The quality papers lauded his business acumen; the tabloids were more interested in promoting his playboy, jet-setting image. Jordan Keston, she mused acidly, apparently had a great many 'close friends' of the petite brunette variety.

'A millionaire at thirty-six...'

She snorted contemptuously, infuriated by the open admiration in Tom's voice. 'And how exactly do you think he's achieved that?' she demanded. 'By utter ruthlessness, by walking over everything and anyone in his path. By using people, playing power games for his own ends.'

'A lot of companies he's taken over were on the brink of collapse,' Tom returned equably. 'He's saved a lot of people's jobs. If he hadn't salvaged Lyne Air Services, you wouldn't be having this interview today,' he added logically.

'St. Jordan to the rescue on his white charger,' Tamsin scoffed, her attention drawn against her will to the sports car again. Two long, lean, dark-trousered legs emerged from the driver's seat, followed by a muscular torso, the expertly tailored jacket doing little to minimize the latent power in the broad shoulders. A breeze ruffled the blue-black hair, and with an impatient gesture he swept back an unruly lock that fell across his forehead.

Jordan Keston, her future employer. Tamsin's eyes glinted with green sparks, her body tensing. Jordan Keston. The man responsible for her parents' divorce. And in three weeks' time he would technically be her stepbrother. A muscle flickered in her small jaw, her teeth clenching together. What was she doing even thinking of accepting a job with him? She couldn't go through with it, couldn't bear to put herself in the position of having to be even remotely grateful to him....

'It's nearly ten to...' she heard Tom remind her from a long way away and mechanically reached for the door handle and scrambled out of the car.

'I'll wait for you in the terminal,' he murmured as he joined her. 'Good luck, Tam.'

She smiled back at him, and was thrown completely off balance as he bent his head abruptly and kissed her resoundingly full on the lips.

She was too startled to even think for a second, and by the time she'd collected herself, he was walking away towards the terminal building. She stared after him with wide, troubled eyes. Tom had never kissed her like that before...just the odd hug, the occasional brotherly peck on the cheek. They were friends, their relationship strictly platonic. She'd never suspected for a moment that he felt anything more towards her. She shook herself. Heck, it had only been a kiss. A one-off.

Her expression pensive, she began to walk across the car park to the Lyne Air Services administration block and then stiffened.

Jordan Keston was standing by his car, watching her, his eyebrows drawn together in an ominous dark line across his forehead, the firm, straight mouth unsmiling, grim disapproval etched into every line of the harsh, uncompromisingly masculine features. She was too far away to see his eyes but she knew instinctively that they would be as bleak, as cold as a winter's sky.

His unrestrained pleasure at seeing her again was hard to take. She tried to grin but her lips wouldn't function as she demanded. What the hell was he looking so disapproving for anyway? Had he witnessed Tom's brief embrace? It had hardly been X-rated, and considering his own lifestyle, certainly didn't warrant such grim censure. Or perhaps it was her mere existence he objected to and was regretting making the job offer that she was fully aware had only been made as an indirect favour to her mother.

Just as she was about to reach him, he stooped, locked the car door, then pulling himself to his full height without even a cursory acknowledgement of her presence, swung on his heel and moved across the gravel with long, fluid strides.

Well, thanks a bunch! Tamsin glowered after his retreating figure. The rude, insufferable oaf. What was he trying to do? Clarify immediately their future roles of employer and employee? Remind her that shortly she would be nothing more than a minnow in the periphery of his immense empire. Snob. Arrogant, condescending snob.

He moved with the easy grace, the controlled power of a feral cat, one part of her mind observed with detachment. And was as equally dangerous and unpredictable, she added mentally. The irrational prickle of fear that suddenly tingled involuntarily down her spine irritated her still further.

She wasn't in awe of Jordan Keston or intimidated by him in any way. His name might be respected on Wall Street but she viewed his business activities as little more than those of an acquisitive, marauding pirate, motivated solely by a ceaseless desire for power. Megalomania. She had, she remembered with a pixie grin, told him so on one occasion. . . .

'Jordan . . .'

From the corner of her eye, Tamsin saw a slender, immaculately groomed, dark-haired woman pick her way delicately across the gravel towards Jordan. Reaching his side, she smiled up into his face, touching his arm with a proprietorial hand, the gesture indicative of familiarity and long acquaintance.

Oh, yuk. Tamsin's mouth turned down with distaste. What a nauseating sight to have to endure at this hour of the morning. The brunette was practically drooling over him. And Jordan, she thought with disdain, judging from that lazy, appreciative smile quirking the corners of his firm mouth, was lapping it up.

She came to an abrupt halt as her heart gave an unexpected twist. She couldn't remember the last time Jordan had actually smiled at her, looked at her with warmth, amusement. . . .

Shaking herself irritably, she propelled herself forward toward the building through which Jordan and his companion had just disappeared. Opening a glass door marked with the Lyne Air logo, she found herself in a small reception area, the smell of paint and pristine cream walls indicating that it had been recently decorated. Jordan was nowhere to be seen, had presumably disappeared behind one of the doors lining the wide corridor ahead.

'May I help you?' The pleasant-faced receptionist glanced up from her typing.

'I have an interview with Jo—Mr. Keston. Tamsin Reed.'

'Oh, yes.' The receptionist checked her name against a list. 'Would you like to take a seat?'

So she wasn't the only interviewee today, Tamsin reflected with surprise as she sat down in a hard-backed chair lined up against the wall. She crossed her slim legs. It seemed a little unfair on the other candidates, not to mention a waste of time, when the position was already taken. Although, of course, she still hadn't made up her mind to accept Jordan's offer, she reminded herself. Working for an airline no one had ever heard of in a small provincial airport was hardly a career move upwards.

She grinned. Now who was sounding arrogant and condescending? And being unemployed was even less of a strategic career move! But not for the first time, she wondered what potential Jordan had seen in the company, especially at a time when so many of its larger competitors were facing difficulties.

Her eyes flicked to the clock on the wall and she uncrossed her legs, her fingers drumming on the arm of the chair. Was Jordan keeping her waiting on purpose? Oh, stick your job—

'Miss Reed?' The receptionist glanced towards her as the intercom buzzed. 'You may go in now. Second door on the left.'

'Thank you.' Unhurriedly, Tamsin rose to her feet and moved down the corridor, uncomfortably aware of just how tenuous was her outward calm. Her mouth was dry, her stomach churning as if she were on a roller coaster.

Oh, for heaven's sake, she chided herself mentally. It was only Jordan behind that door, the interview itself a complete charade. She swallowed. That was the trouble. Jordan. She only had to look at him, hear his voice, and a scorching blaze of antagonism would fire through her. Everything about him grated on her, had from the moment she'd first laid eyes on him. His raw, aggressive masculinity, his unassailable confidence, his arrogant assumption that he only had to click his fingers and everyone would jump to obey his imperial commands.

She eyed the closed door and her small chin squared resolutely. Well, this was one puppet who wasn't going to jump when he pulled the strings. He wasn't going to rattle her or play any of his overbearing power games with her today. Or think she was going to do a grovelling, grateful routine for his largesse in giving her a job. As far as she was concerned, he would be damn lucky to have her on his staff.

A brisk, confident smile on her lips, she pushed open the door and faltered. Jordan, his face an expressionless granite mask, was sitting behind a large oak desk, and next to him was the brunette with whom she'd seen him earlier.

'Good morning, Miss Reed.' His voice was cool and impersonal. 'Please sit down.' The blue eyes swept over her with clinical detachment.

Miss Reed? Tamsin gazed back at him in disbelief. He was treating her, looking at her—no, assessing her—as if she were a total stranger. As if this were a genuine interview....

'What the hell are you playing at, Jordan?' She swallowed the words before they formed on her lip, conscious of and inhibited by the other woman's presence.

Who on earth was she anyway? Jordan's latest 'insep-
arable companion'? she wondered caustically. If she
moved any closer, she'd be practically sitting in his lap.

'Sara Lyne.'

Tamsin's eyebrows shot up as Jordan made the brief
introduction. Lyne? As in Lyne Air? Or mere coincidence? Moving across the carpet to the chair placed stra-
tegically in front of the table, Tamsin exchanged cool
smiles with the other woman. Attractive in rather an obvious sort of way. Pity about that particular shade of
lipstick. She was slightly appalled at the surge of antipathy that tore through her towards a woman with whom
she'd yet to exchange two words.

'You have worked in the field of aviation for the past
five years, since you were eighteen?' Jordan began
without preamble the moment she was seated. He leaned
back in his own chair as he surveyed her, the movement
causing the dark jacket to tauten across his powerful
shoulders. A ray of sun filtered into the room, danced
over the thick, dark hair.

Tamsin focused her eyes at a point above his head.
'Yes,' she agreed with barely veiled exasperation. This
was becoming more and more absurd. He knew damn
well she had. Her eyes flicked back to his face, traced
the line of the tenacious jaw, encompassed the hard,
cynical mouth and the square, decisive chin. He would
need to shave at least twice a day to avoid six o'clock
shadow, she thought inconsequentially as her sense of
smell was teased by the faint, subtle fragrance of expensive male aftershave.

'As you can see from my c.v.,' she said with deliberate
innocence, addressing his left lapel, 'I joined the
company initially as a seasonal traffic assistant, was then

offered a permanent position in Reservations where I spent—'

'But you were only directly involved with Operations for two of those years?' he cut through with ill-concealed impatience.

Tamsin's eyes glinted. How a courteous man like Andrew Keston could have sired such an offspring was one of the wonders of the modern world. 'Yes,' she said tightly.

Her gaze fell to the table. One lean hand rested palm downwards in front of her eyes, the strong, supple fingers splayed across a pile of papers. A sprinkle of fine dark hair covered the tanned wrist revealed below the cuff of the brilliant white shirt. Disconcerted and infuriated at the way her stomach suddenly dipped, Tamsin stared resolutely down at the carpet, forcing herself to concentrate on the deep, assured voice.

'Lyne Air commenced operations some fifteen years ago, primarily as a charter company. Four years ago, the company entered into a franchise agreement with one of the major airlines, operating various scheduled domestic and European services on their behalf. Very shortly, Lyne Air will be operating these services under its own route licence and flight numbers, undertaking its own handling completely.' He paused. 'Do you feel that with your limited operations experience, you are sufficiently qualified not simply to assist in running an existing department but to help reorganize its basic structure? Retrain staff? Recruit new staff as necessary?'

'Yes, I do,' Tamsin assured the carpet confidently.

'Well, frankly, I do not.'

'What?' Tamsin's head jerked up, her eyes flying to his face. She'd risen at the crack of dawn, come all the way down from London to be told within the space of two minutes that she didn't have the necessary qualifications for a job that she'd already been offered! He couldn't possibly be serious. This was simply an example of his warped sense of humour. He was deliberately trying to wind her up....

The hard, flagrantly male features were as unyielding as rock, the firm mouth drawn into a tough, uncompromising straight line. Her eyes locked into the dark blue ones, searched their fathomless depths. They were devoid of all warmth or humour, detached, indifferent. He was serious.

Jordan had never intended offering her the job of senior duty officer. He'd been playing one of his power games from the start, though to what end she couldn't even begin to comprehend. But then, when had she ever been able to understand this cold-blooded, devious, manipulative, power-crazy excuse for a human being? She fought back the smouldering anger that threatened to engulf her completely, refused to allow anything Jordan did or said provoke her into losing her temper. Fight ice with ice. How could she have been so stupid, so naïve as to have let him dupe her yet again, to have trusted him, believed a word he said? Well, to hell with Jordan Keston! And to hell with his tinpot airline—

'Sit down. I haven't finished.'

The low-timbred voice halted her as she began to rise to her feet.

'Really?' she enquired coolly, amazed at the control in her voice. She wanted to pummel that hard, deep chest, yell at him. 'Well, I have. You may have time to waste. I don't.'

'Sit down,' Jordan repeated quietly. His eyes sought and held hers, and to her chagrin and disbelief, Tamsin found herself sinking back into the chair as if some part of her over which she had no control was acquiescing instinctively to his authority. 'However,' he continued smoothly as if there had been no interruption, 'although I don't feel that you have the necessary qualifications for senior duty officer, there is another vacancy within the company for which you may wish to be considered.'

Tamsin's eyes darkened suspiciously as he paused, but she couldn't stop the pinprick of curiosity.

'We are looking for someone with a wide, all-round airline experience, not necessarily expertise in any one field, to assist in Operations, Traffic, Reservations when there is an increased workload in any of those departments. To cover sickness, leave.' He swivelled sideways in his chair away from the desk, stretching out cramped, lean legs in front of him. 'The position would be a temporary one initially, reviewable at the end of the season.' He named a salary that was fair if not lavish, and then catching Tamsin totally off guard, enquired curtly, 'Any questions?' Giving her no time to conjure up one out of her suddenly blank mind, he bent his head over the pile of papers in front of him. 'Right, thank you, Miss Reed,' he said dismissively without glancing up again. 'We'll be in touch in due course.'

Slowly, Tamsin rose to her feet, a feeling of complete unreality engulfing her as she walked across the room to the door. Nodding absently to the secretary, she stepped out into the sunshine, came to an abrupt halt and burst into laughter, the tension easing from her body.

From senior duty officer to general dogsbody—and a temporary one at that—within the space of five minutes.

And even then he hadn't actually confirmed that the job was hers. She'd allowed Jordan to dominate her completely. Except for a brief minor rebellion, which he'd quickly squashed, she'd just sat there. Meekly. Like a lump of passive jelly. Had barely spoken two words.

She began to walk towards the terminal building. Well, that was two more than Sara Lyne, she reminded herself. The brunette hadn't spoken once—her whole attention, like her own, had been focused on Jordan. She grinned. So Jordan liked his women small, dark—and silent! The smile stiffened on her lips and she kicked a pebble ferociously with her foot, her eyes dark amber. What malevolent quirk of fate had ever brought Jordan Keston into her life? she wondered despondently. If only she had been cycling down that lane a few seconds earlier, a few seconds later... She'd been so happy that summer's evening, four years ago. It had been her nineteenth birthday and she'd been spending a few days' leave with her mother in the family home in Berkshire....

Tamsin's long, gleaming brown hair cascaded over her bare golden shoulders as her tanned legs whisked at the pedals of her old bicycle. It had been a glorious day. In fact it was a glorious, wonderful life. Her mouth curved in a wide smile of pure contentment. Would her father still be there when she arrived home?

The celebratory birthday lunch to which her father had been invited at her insistence had been more of a success than she'd dared hope for. It had almost been like old times, her parents laughing and teasing each other, reminiscing. Neither had her father appeared to be in any rush to depart after lunch, so tactfully disappearing for the evening to visit an old school friend had seemed the least she could do.

Her smile widened. Everything was going to be all right. Her parents had finally come to their senses after all these months of separation, and a reconciliation was in the offing. She was convinced of it.

Humming under her breath, she free-wheeled down the steep, winding hill, revelling in the speed, the rush of sweet-scented, late-evening air on her heated skin. She rounded a bend, saw the dark green Land Rover, heard the squeal of brakes... then everything became totally confused. She was lying in the ditch, winded, her head spinning.

'You damn little fool. You could have been killed... cycling in the middle of the road, out of control...'

From a long way away, she heard the deep, irate voice, was vaguely aware that someone was kneeling over her. Her dark lashes flicking upwards, she looked up dazedly into a pair of furious blue eyes, received a hazy, blurred impression of hard, aggressive male features.

'You were driving like a maniac,' she retaliated automatically but without much conviction. Her head was still whizzing round and she felt sick. 'Far too fast for these narrow country lanes,' she rambled and then broke off, gasping with shocked surprise as she felt warm male fingers sliding over her arms, moving slowly over the contours of her body, trailing the length of her bare leg. 'Get your filthy hands off me.' Adrenalin surging through her, she forced herself into a sitting position. 'You nearly run me over and now...' She was suddenly conscious of her isolation, the encroaching dusk. Her hands clenched together. 'You damn pervert!' She slammed her small fist upwards and caught him on the jaw, wincing with pain as her knuckles encountered hard muscle.

Caught totally off guard, the man reeled back on his haunches, the expression of incredulity on his face almost making her burst into laughter. Almost. Taking full advantage of his temporary distraction, she began to struggle to her feet.

'Are you all right, my dear?'

She spun round, relief flooding her as she saw the tall, grey-haired man approaching her, kindly concern etched on his face. Then came the realization that this man must have been a passenger in the Land Rover, was probably tarred with the same brush. Her hands clenched again.

'No, you don't, you crazy little...' firm fingers closed around her arm like a steel trap, holding her immobile. 'No bones broken. Grazed elbow. The only real damage appears to be to her head,' the man towering over her murmured laconically.

She? He was talking about her as if she wasn't there, as if she were a child, Tamsin registered as she tried vainly to wrench herself away from his vicelike grip.

'Would you please let me go, you damn great bully?' she demanded savagely. Tilting her head upwards, she appraised her captor fully for the first time. There was something oddly familiar about the harshly chiselled male features, the tenacious angle of the square chin, the dark, unreadable blue eyes. Yet she was certain she had never met him before. The sleeves of his navy blue shirt were folded back to reveal strong, tanned forearms; close-fitting, faded denims were moulded to the narrow hips, powerful thighs and long, lean legs. He was not a man, she admitted grudgingly, that she would be likely to forget.

'Only if you promise not to slug me again,' he drawled. 'Next time you might lay me out cold.'

Despite herself, the sheer absurdity of his words made her lips twitch. This man looked tough, resourceful, more than capable of handling any situation in which he found himself. At the same time, some instinct told her that he would never physically hurt anything smaller or weaker than himself. Neither, she was certain, some deep, feminine part of her acknowledging that masculine assurance, would he ever need to force his unwanted attentions on any woman.

He released her arm and rubbed his jaw with a lean hand. 'Next time, pick on someone your own size, hmm?'

Very droll! The patronizing amusement in his voice made her hackles rise. She could have dealt with his anger far more easily. A fact, the taunting glint in the astute blue eyes informed her, of which he was fully aware. She regarded him disdainfully, vaguely conscious that the older man had walked across to retrieve her bike and shoulder-bag from the ditch.

'All right, perhaps I did overreact slightly,' she conceded coolly, 'but what was I supposed to think when a total stranger starts pawing me?'

He smiled. 'I have never ''pawed'' a woman in my life,' he murmured in a low, silky voice, and to Tamsin's incredulity, she blushed at the sudden unwanted images exploding in her head. This man would seduce a woman subtly, skilfully... Oh, God, she must have knocked her head after all.

She turned with relief to the older man as he joined them.

'Back wheel's buckled, I'm afraid,' he said with a gentle smile, giving her the shoulder-bag. 'Andrew Keston,' he added, holding out a hand.

Keston? Her mind whizzed as she shook his outstretched hand and introduced herself, recognition dawning as she shot a glance up at the man looming by her side. Jordan Keston. Of course. The business tycoon. It was practically impossible to pick up a newspaper without seeing him plastered across it.

She saw the blue eyes narrow abruptly, a shuttered mask slam down over his face. Turning away, he took hold of the bike from his father and tossed it easily into the back of the Land Rover. 'Where do you live, Miss Reed?'

The brusqueness in his deep-timbred voice, the cold indifference as he glanced over his broad shoulder flicked her on the raw. Now that she knew his identity, it was almost as if he was expecting her to turn into some creeping sycophant and was warning her off.

'I'm quite capable of making my own way home,' she said icily. Of all the shallow, egoistical... 'Although doubtless it would ease your conscience to give me a lift,' she added sweetly and scowled at the unresponsive muscled back.

'I think the sooner your elbow is attended to, the better,' Andrew Keston cut in softly, propelling her gently but firmly towards the Land Rover.

Frowning, Tamsin looked down and saw the blood trickling over her arm. Nausea ripped her throat and she gritted her teeth, fighting against the grey, swirling mist. She could hear the murmur of male voices but couldn't distinguish the words as she desperately tried to claw her way out of the darkness that threatened to engulf her completely.

Tamsin's eyes flickered open and she frowned, disorientated as she stared up at the familiar ceiling. What exactly was she doing lying on the chesterfield in the sitting room with a rug tucked around her? She turned her head and jolted at the disconcerting sight of Jordan Keston sitting, long legs stretched out indolently in front of him, in the armchair opposite her. And what exactly was *he* doing here?

'You fainted,' he drawled lazily, his eyes, dark, opaque blue pools, focused on her face.

Her gaze flew to her arm. She saw the small sticking-plaster on her elbow and groaned inwardly. Oh, God, barely a scratch, little more than a graze and she had—

'Your mother explained.'

'Did she?' she said shortly, her small chin squaring pugnaciously. OK. Laugh. It made her sound so utterly feeble, like a drooping Victorian heroine. Swooning at the sight of her own blood. And it was a phobia she had thought she'd finally overcome.

What a pathetic, neurotic idiot he must think her. Her jaw clenched. Who cared? He looked as if he owned the damned place, she thought with a surge of resentment, legs sprawled out in front of him, hands folded idly behind his dark head.

'How did you know—'

'Looked in your shoulder-bag,' he cut in laconically. 'Found your address on some library tickets.'

'You had no right,' she flashed and then closed her mouth, recognizing that he'd had no alternative. It was also fortunate that the old library tickets had her family address on them rather than the flat in Croydon. She ran a hand through her hair, tucking it behind her ears. She supposed she ought to thank him for bringing her home, she admitted grudgingly. But the words stuck in her throat.

She suddenly felt stifled, the large, beautifully proportioned room claustrophobic. Abruptly she flung back the rug, swinging herself into a sitting position, her feminine pride oddly piqued that there wasn't the slightest flicker of male appreciation at the length of smooth, tanned leg revealed by the action. His face remained completely impassive. Yet, perversely, she admitted honestly, if he had evinced the slightest interest, she would have been equally irritated.

'Where's my mother?'

He lifted a dark eyebrow in the direction of the French windows. 'Showing my father the garden.' The straight mouth quirked. 'Fellow rose buffs.'

'Really?' Tamsin said coolly, frowning as the sound of Andrew's soft voice, followed by her mother's unmistakable, attractive laugh, floated into the room. Rising to her feet, she watched her mother walk towards the house, her head tilted up towards the grey-haired man by her side, her face animated. Clad in a faded summer dress, her fair hair cut in a flattering bob, she looked absurdly young and happy.

Spinning round, Tamsin surveyed the lounging figure. 'Now you've done your Sir Galahad routine, shouldn't you be galloping off into the sunset?' she enquired sweetly. Pointedly, she glanced at the clock on the mantelpiece. 'Have you far to go?' With every fibre in her being, she suddenly wanted Jordan Keston and his father

gone. Out of the house. Preferably to the other side of
the world. Never wanted to lay eyes on either of them
again as long as she lived.

'Not far,' he drawled, and with a lazy smile crossed
one lean leg over the other, settling back even more
comfortably into the chair. 'I moved into Swallow Lodge
this morning.'

'What?' Tamsin looked at him incredulously. She had
witnessed the renovation taking place on the Lodge over
the past few months and like her mother had been intrigued to know who had bought the beautiful old house
set in the spacious grounds with the river frontage.

But Jordan Keston…a virtual neighbour. As the dark
eyes drew and held hers, she felt an icy finger trail down
her spine and an illogical, irrational feeling of fore-
boding twisting deep inside her.

CHAPTER TWO

IT WAS as if she'd had a premonition, had known in that second that nothing would ever be the same again, Tamsin mused gloomily as she approached the passenger terminal. It was disturbing, too, to realize that where Jordan was concerned she seemed to have almost total recall, could even after all this time, remember virtually every detail of their first encounter.

The automatic doors slid open in front of her and she stepped through, surprised to discover just how deceptive was the building from the outside. Skilful use of colour and modern refurbishments created a pleasing illusion of light and space. She walked past the line of check-in desks towards the clearly marked self-service cafeteria and found Tom sitting at a table, empty cup in front of him, gazing out of the huge windows that overlooked the airfield, watching a light aircraft coming in to land.

'That must be the shortest interview on record!' he exclaimed with a welcoming grin as she reached him.

Tamsin grinned back, relieved that he showed no signs of embarrassment or awkwardness at seeing her, confirming that his impromptu kiss had been as unimportant and as meaningless as she'd hoped.

'Like a coffee?'

She shook her head. 'Perhaps we could stop off somewhere on the way back,' she suggested, suddenly longing to leave the airport, to put as much distance between herself and Jordan as possible.

Yet it hadn't always been like that, she reflected a short time later as Tom manoeuvred the car into the steady stream of traffic heading towards London. There had been a time, she remembered with an unexpected ache, that she'd actually enjoyed his company, had looked forward to seeing him. Had, she reminded herself with self-disgust, been totally duped by his superficial charm.

It had been two days after she'd first met him that Jordan had telephoned. Her initial surprise at hearing the deep, assured voice had changed to suspicion and bafflement when he'd invited her to a barbecue at Swallow Lodge that evening. Her instinct had been to refuse, convinced that he had no more desire to further their acquaintance than she had.

But to her disbelief she had heard herself accepting, later telling herself that she'd been motivated purely by curiosity, intrigued to see the renovations that had been carried out on Swallow Lodge. It had seemed almost as an afterthought, she mused wryly, that Jordan had suggested that her mother might like to be included in the invitation.

Jordan had been the perfect host that evening. Courteous, considerate, entertaining. She'd actually convinced herself that she had misjudged him on their first encounter, and when he'd casually extended an open invitation to use the swimming pool and tennis court, she'd been conscious of a warm glow of tingling happiness. It had hardly registered at the time that he'd proffered a similar invitation to her mother... Or that Andrew was staying temporarily at Swallow Lodge....

It had been a perfect summer and she'd escaped from London at every opportunity. Her eyes darkened to amber as the images slowly unfurled in her head. Long, hot days lazing around the pool at Swallow Lodge with Jordan, Andrew and her mother. Golden evenings playing tennis with Jordan. Jordan teaching her to row on the river. Jordan laughing down at her, teasing her. And always in the background, her mother and Andrew...

Disbelievingly, Tamsin shook her head from side to side as she looked back over the years. Had it never once occurred to her all that glorious summer to wonder why a man like Jordan Keston should be spending so much time with an unsophisticated, immature nineteen-year-old, her mother and his father? How could she have been so dense, so gullible as not to see what was going on right in front of her eyes? Or had she seen it and simply refused to accept it?

The realization had dawned like a bombshell. She'd driven down to Berkshire for one of her precious weekends off to discover Swallow Lodge closed up and shuttered, to learn from her mother that Jordan had gone back to New York. For an indefinite period. Her mother had then added diffidently that Andrew had invited her out to dinner that evening. That had marked the start of Andrew's long, old-fashioned courtship, culminating in his proposal six months ago.

She hadn't seen Jordan for over a year and it had been like meeting a stranger. He'd been distant, cold, remote. But then she'd been of no further use to him, she reminded herself caustically. He no longer needed her as an unwitting pawn in his little game. The merger between their respective parents had been successfully accomplished. . . .

'Would you like that coffee or prefer to sit here and day-dream?'

As Tom's teasing voice broke through her reverie, she realized with a jolt that he had drawn up in front of a service station. Returning his grin, she reached for the door handle, firmly pushing the uneasy, unwelcome memories to the back of her mind.

Kneeling on the floor of her bedroom, Tamsin strapped up the packing case in front of her and stood up. It was over a week since her interview and she hadn't heard a word from Jordan. Wiping a grimy hand down her blue sweatshirt and faded jeans, she grimaced at the bare wall in front of her.

Jordan was a man accustomed to making important snap judgements every day of his life—and after ten days he still hadn't reached a decision about a minor, temporary position within his latest acquisition? She didn't believe it. He was deliberately stringing her along. Well, she most certainly wasn't going to play right into his hands by contacting him.

She glanced up as Tom appeared around the door, her pony-tail swinging over her shoulder. 'Is that the lot?' he asked.

She nodded as he picked up the case. 'I didn't realize how much stuff I'd left here,' she said ruefully. She started to follow him from the room and stopped, turning round in the doorway. Slowly her gaze moved around the bedroom, now empty of everything but the basic furniture, and her throat constricted. Although she had moved to the flat in Croydon four years ago, this house had still been her home. Every room in it was redolent of her childhood, her teenage years...her father...

She padded across to the window and stared out. And now the house was sold, the removal men arriving on Monday, and she would walk out of the front door for the last time. That gnawing ache that had been with her constantly over the past two days spent helping her mother pack the house contents intensified. Pulling up the sash window, she leaned out and, craning her neck, glimpsed the gabled roof of Swallow Lodge through a gap in the trees. Her mother would be staying there in the luxurious guest suite until after the wedding, then, after an extended honeymoon, moving into a house in Maidenhead with her new husband.

Tamsin's hands clenched by her side. Maybe her parents would never have been reunited, but whatever hope there had been had been destroyed the day Jordan Keston moved into Swallow Lodge.

Jerkily, she fished into the back pocket of her jeans and retrieved the photograph she'd discovered that morning pushed to the back of a drawer in her dressing table. She couldn't even remember who had taken it, or why she'd kept it. Eyes narrowed, she stared down at the colour print. Jordan, clad in faded denims and black T-shirt, arms folded indolently across his chest, smiled lazily into the camera. Next to him stood a long-legged, nineteen-year-old girl, gazing not at the photographer but up at the man towering by her side. And the expression in those hazel eyes made her wince.

Abruptly, she tossed the photograph into the black refuse bag in the corner of the room and walked briskly out of the door in search of Tom, discovering him in the drive, stowing her cases in the boot of the car.

'Are you sure you won't stay for lunch?' she asked as he slammed the boot shut. She still felt guilty that he had given up his Saturday morning to come over and transport her belongings back to Croydon. But she hadn't asked him, she reminded herself. He had offered. No more than that. Insisted.

He shook his head and glanced at his wristwatch. 'No, I'd better get a move on. Can't be late for the last match of the season.' He passed. 'Sure you won't come and watch? It won't be the same without you hollering from the touch-line.'

Tamsin grinned. 'Sorry, Tom,' she said regretfully, 'but there's still so much to do.'

'How about going out for a pizza this evening, then? I'll come over and pick you up.'

'OK,' Tamsin agreed. 'But I'll catch the train or borrow Mum's car and meet you back at the flat about eight. And it's my treat,' she added firmly. It was the least she could do to thank him for all his good-natured help—although it would make even more inroads into her savings.

She stepped back as Tom opened the door and slid into the driver's seat, was about to turn back into the house when he wound down the window. 'This came for you yesterday.' He pulled out a letter from his pocket and handed it to her. 'Sorry. Forgot. Lyne Air?'

Tamsin nodded as she tore open the envelope and scanned its contents. Tom had been carrying the letter around with him all morning....

'Well?'

'I've been offered the job. To start a week Monday.' The sight of Jordan's distinctive signature on the formal, succinct letter triggered off a spark of irritation. Couldn't he have just picked up the phone and offered her the job verbally? But then that would have necessitated having direct contact with her, she reminded herself caustically, something he avoided as much as possible these days.

'And you're going to take it? Move out of the flat?'

She frowned, puzzled by the flatness in Tom's voice, the expression on his face. 'I don't have much choice. I—'

'See you tonight,' Tom cut through before she had time to finish and, turning on the ignition, reversed swiftly out of the drive. Eyebrows drawn together, Tamsin retraced her steps to the house, mulling over Tom's inexplicable behaviour. He had known she was waiting for that letter... why hadn't he called her yesterday to tell her it had arrived? He'd seemed so reluctant to give it to her. And he hadn't even congratulated her....

Closing the front door, she started down the hall towards the kitchen then paused, catching a glimpse of her mother through the open doorway of the dining room. Surrounded by packing cases, she was staring bleakly at the empty wall in front of her. Even though it had been her own choice to sell the house to which she'd first come as a young bride, the past few days must have been as painful and difficult for her mother as for herself, Tamsin recognized uncomfortably. Probably more so.

She longed to throw her arms around her mother, tell her she understood, but held back. Although superficially the same, her relationship with her mother, once very close, had altered over the past few years. There was now a gap between them, unspecified but ever widening.

Tamsin cleared her throat. 'Mum? Fancy a sandwich?'

Instantly, her mother's expression changed, resumed its normal serenity. 'That would be lovely, darling.' She looked down ruefully at her dusty hands as she moved into the hall. 'I'll just go and have a quick wash.' She started up the stairs and paused as the doorbell rang. 'Oh, Lord, who can that be?'

'I'll go.' Pushing back an errant lock of silky hair that had escaped the confines of her pony-tail, Tamsin crossed the hall and opened the front door. 'Jordan...'

Caught totally off guard by his unexpected appearance, her stomach muscles clenched in an immediate and instinctive feminine response to his maleness as he towered over her, denims clinging to lean hips, brown leather jacket hugging the broad shoulders.

'What do you want?' she enquired frigidly, infuriated by her initial reaction to him. Other women went weak in the knees and in the head at the sight of Jordan Keston. Not her. Never her. His brand of blatant, raw masculinity had no appeal for her. She was completely immune to him.

'Is your mother here?' he enquired brusquely and before she had time to answer stepped over the threshold.

'Do come in,' Tamsin muttered caustically. She turned to close the door, but Jordan was ahead of her and it took every ounce of control not to snatch her hand away as it encountered the firm strong fingers instead of the expected doorknob.

'Where's your mother?' Jordan repeated tersely.

'Sh-she's upstairs....' Her fingers had barely brushed his and yet her whole hand was tingling, warmth teasing up her arm.

'Would you go and tell her I'm here, please,' he demanded curtly.

Instantly, her hackles rose at his pre-emptive tone, the barely disguised command. He hadn't even greeted her by name, had barely glanced at her.

'She'll be down in a minute,' she said coolly. 'We were just about to have lunch,' she continued pointedly, walking away towards the kitchen. 'You can wait in the sitting room if you like,' she threw back over her shoulder offhandedly. If she had treated a guest like this as a child, her parents would have reprimanded her for her ill manners, a voice in the back of her head informed her. She dismissed it. Jordan Keston didn't deserve civility.

'Don't you think it's time we stopped fighting, Tamsin? Called a truce?'

The quiet, low voice stopped her in her tracks, his words catching her completely off balance. Eyebrows knitted together in a tiny suspicious frown, she turned round slowly and surveyed the lean figure leaning against the closed door, arms folded indolently across his deep chest. Jordan Keston in the role of peacemaker? The strong, assured face was a mask, his eyes unreadable.

'So how about it, Tamsin?' he continued softly, moving silently across the carpet towards her. 'Friends?'

She shrugged her slim shoulders, conscious of her stomach dipping as she tilted her head upwards to meet his gaze. A truce? Jordan as a friend? No more animosity. Nor more of his taunts. To feel comfortable and at ease in his presence. Was it possible?

He was so close she could smell the minty toothpaste freshness of his breath mingled with the scent of clean, soapy male skin. He must have showered recently, one part of her mind registered. His hair still looked faintly damp, springing up from his head in thick, dark waves. Her throat constricted. What would it be like to slide her fingers through that thick richness?

'Four years is a long time to hold a grudge, Tamsin. Don't you think it's time to forgive me?'

The dark-lashed blue eyes were beginning to mesmerize her, make her feel disorientated. She tried to break his gaze but seemed powerless to do so, was appalled at the way her heart was hammering beneath her ribcage. 'Forgive you?' she repeated huskily.

'For rejecting you. For not taking a frustrated nineteen-year-old virgin to my bed four years ago.'

Tamsin went rigid, shock waves of revulsion crawling down her spine as she met the narrowed, taunting eyes. How could she have been so gullible, so dense as to seriously believe for one second that Jordan was extending an olive branch? 'You are the most disgusting—'

'Hell hath no fury,' the deep voice drawled mockingly as he ably caught hold of her hand before it had reached its intended target. 'Perhaps if you hadn't been quite so obvious, so eager...' Azure eyes moved over her flushed face and dropped with deliberate insolence to the swell of her breasts rising and falling in time to her erratic breathing. 'I like my women to be a little more subtle, more of a challenge. I bought Swallow Lodge as a retreat and every time I turned round, you were there—'

'You arrogant bastard!' Wrenching her hand free, Tamsin looked at him contemptuously, eyes sparking with golden flames. 'I hate to spoil your egotistical little fantasy, Jordan, but the only attraction Swallow Lodge had for me that summer was the swimming pool and tennis court. Then and now.'

'Really, Tamsin?' Raising a thoughtful dark eyebrow, he moved towards her and laughed mockingly as she took an instinctive step backwards. 'So why is it that every time I come anywhere near you, you flee like a terrified mouse? What are you so frightened of?'

Tamsin took a deep, controlling breath, wondering what perverseness made her feel more angry to be likened to a timid rodent than virtually being accused of latent nymphomania! 'I suppose it hasn't occurred to you that I simply dislike your company?' She smiled. 'That you bore me?'

Jordan smiled back. 'So I bore you, hmm?' he murmured silkily, moving towards her again.

This time she stood her ground but was conscious of a totally irrational prickle of fear tingling down her spine. Even more disturbing was her total awareness of his proximity, every nerve ending in her body alive, responding against her will to his dominant maleness. Schooling her features into an impassive mask, she tilted her head upwards. 'Yes, you do. Infinitely,' she agreed sweetly and faltered, her eyes dilating as she saw his gaze drop speculatively to the curve of her mouth.

He wouldn't dare... He was simply baiting her, trying to intimidate her and it wouldn't work. She swallowed. 'And now if you'll excuse me,' she murmured with exaggerated politeness, turning away, 'I really am very busy— Jordan!'

Every muscle in her body contracted as his hand clamped down on her shoulder and swung her round.

'W-would you let me go?' she demanded jerkily, panic swelling up inside her as his other hand curved round the back of her head, holding her immobile. His fingers were sliding through her hair, massaging her scalp in slow, sensuous circles, sending tiny shivers down her spine.

'Jordan . . . let me go. . . .' The words came out as no more than a whisper as his lips brushed her forehead, moved slowly over her cheekbones.

What was she doing? she thought frantically, standing there passively, unresistingly. She should be protesting, pushing him away with all her force. She raised her hands and they fell back weakly to her side as his lips trailed a sensual path to her ear, teasing the delicate whorls with an expert tongue. She couldn't seem to think coherently, seemed to have lost all will-power, was slipping mindlessly into a bath of warm, sensuous pleasure as his mouth slid down her neck and closed over the pulse beating erratically at the base of her throat.

As the firm, hard mouth finally took possession of hers, she shuddered, her eyelashes flickering downwards, her hands of their own volition moving upwards to curl around Jordan's neck. There was nothing in the world but this man and that aching need inside her. . . .

'Still bored?'

Slowly, the mocking voice penetrated through the haze. Dazedly, she opened her eyes and, as she met the hard, disdainful blue ones, witnessed the mocking satisfaction in their depths, felt as if she'd been douched with cold water. It had been nothing more than a game to him. There had been no warmth, feeling, not even momentary desire in his caresses.

He'd executed his mini seduction with the cold, detached calculation of a machine, as if she'd been nothing more than a lump of wood. And she had responded, she thought with searing humiliation, her body firing with cringing heat. Had for a few irretrievable seconds completely lost her senses.

Her stomach muscles cramped in a sick knot. She wanted to lash out, scream her protest, but that would be playing right into Jordan's hands. Summonsing every ounce of will-power, she surveyed him with cool, unwavering eyes, and then slowly and deliberately wiped her mouth with the back of her hand.

'I like *my* men to be warm, compassionate human beings. Not cold-blooded automatons.'

He raised a thoughtful dark eyebrow and smiled. 'And have there been many men, Tamsin?' he enquired softly.

Tamsin shrugged, envisaging his derision if he knew just how limited was her experience of men. 'I hardly think that is any of your bus—'

The words died in her throat as, giving her no warning of his intention, Jordan snaked out a hand and drew her effortlessly against him, the hard mouth coming down on hers in a ruthless, punishing onslaught. There was no slow rising of warmth, just an explosion of senses. She could hardly breathe, his mouth grinding her lips against her teeth, which were clenched together in a desperate attempt to repel a deeper unwanted intimacy.

Her breasts were crushed against the unyielding wall of his chest, her slender thighs moulded to the hard male contours. She could hear a roaring in her ears, feel the blood scorching through her veins.

His release was as sudden as had been the violation, left her disorientated and confused, drawing deep gulps of air into her lungs. Then the anger ignited inside her. Her eyes, sparking with golden fire, leaped to his face, and she faltered, the torrent of furious words drowning in her throat.

There was no trace of mockery or complacent victory on his face. His eyes beneath the thick, dark lashes were warm, navy blue pools, the corners of the straight mouth quirking into a slow, lazy smile that instantly softened the harsh male features.

Her stomach dipped without warning. It had been years since Jordan had looked at her like that, had actually smiled at her. She tried desperately hard to hold on to her anger but could feel it draining from her body. She felt weak and uncertain, strangely light-headed. Then she froze, realization hitting her like a physical blow. Jordan's gaze wasn't directed at her but over her shoulder. Jerking her head around, she saw her mother descending the stairs.

'Anne.'

Incredulously, she watched as Jordan moved smoothly past her and greeted her mother with a kiss on the cheek. He looked as controlled, as assured as if he had just spent the past few minutes discussing the weather. Unconsciously, her hands clenched into fists, the nails biting painfully into the soft palms. He'd completely forgotten her existence, dismissing her instantly as if she were of no consequence at all. She welcomed the renewed surge of anger because it camouflaged the far more disturbing emotions churning inside her.

As if she were in a bubble, curiously isolated from her surroundings, she saw Jordan take hold of her mother's hand, heard the murmur of the deep-timbred voice without registering the words. Why hadn't she protested the moment he'd touched her? she berated herself savagely. She must have been mad, temporarily insane— She jerked as her mother's bewildered, agitated voice penetrated through the bubble.

'Andrew? Appendicitis? But he can't have... he's in Geneva on a business trip for you... he phoned last night and he was fine....'

'He was taken into hospital late last night,' Jordan said quietly, 'and went into the operating theatre first thing this morning. It was a complete success.'

My God! Tamsin's eyes raked over the harsh contours of Jordan's face, disgust welling up inside her. All the time he'd been indulging in his puerile game, his father was lying in hospital. The man was inhuman, incapable of normal, decent behaviour.

'But why didn't you let me know earlier...?'

Tamsin saw a muscle flicker along the line of Jordan's tenacious jaw. 'I've only just received the message myself from my Swiss office, Anne.' He paused almost imperceptibly. 'I've been... unattainable since yesterday evening.'

Jordan Keston unattainable? Without a contact number? Tamsin's throat tightened. The entrepreneur millionaire with every form of modern telecommunications at his fingertip, who in all the time she'd known him had never been more than an arm's reach from a telephone in the advent of a crisis occurring in his vast empire, incommunicado? Without warning, an image of Sara Lyne floated into her head. She dismissed it furiously. She didn't care a damn how or with whom Jordan spent his leisure hours. And all that mattered right now was Andrew and her mother.

'He'll be all right, Mum.' She moved to her mother's side and placed an arm around her shoulder, then raised a stony face to Jordan. Now he had played messenger boy, couldn't he just go and leave them alone?

There wasn't a trace of emotion on those hard, chiselled features. Not even a hint of anxiety or concern, Tamsin registered incredulously. His face was a bland mask, his eyes unreadable. The man was made of ice, incapable of feeling anything for anyone, even his own father.

As if sensing her scrutiny, his gaze flicked to her face, and for a brief second, blue eyes locked into the frozen hazel ones. The corners of the straight mouth suddenly twitched, making her infuriatingly aware that, far from being disconcerted by her unspoken censure, he was merely amused by it.

'May I use the telephone?' His gaze moved back to the older woman, and receiving the affirmation, he moved purposefully across the hall.

Tamsin frowned, eyes narrowing as they rested speculatively on the broad back, aware that her mother's attention like her own was focused on Jordan. They were both standing there like mindless puppets awaiting their cue from him, as if they'd completely lost the ability to act on their own initiative.

Shaking herself roughly, Tamsin placed a hand on her mother's arm and steered her gently into the kitchen. 'Come on, Mum, let's have lunch.' Uneasily, she recognized how instinctive it would always be to allow Jordan to take command in any crisis, to bow without question to his authority and judgement.

'I'm not very hungry,' her mother murmured, absently sinking into a chair beside the round pine table. Packing cases lined the far wall with the bulk of the kitchen crockery and utensils. 'If only he was nearer...' her voice trailed off.

Switching on the kettle, Tamsin extracted a loaf of bread from the bin. As soon as Jordan had finished with the telephone, she would call the local travel agent and find out the times of flights to Geneva, arrange hotel accommodation. Blue the rest of her savings. Present her mother with a *fait accompli*.

She sensed Jordan's presence the minute he entered the kitchen. Fingers tightening around the bread knife, she flicked a quick glance over her shoulder and saw him blocking the open doorway, the dark blue eyes directed towards her mother.

'Foxtrot Lima is on standby at Heathrow with a current slot time of 1430,' he stated without preamble. 'As soon as you're ready, Anne, I'll run you to the airport. I've arranged for a driver to be at your disposal when you arrive in Geneva and made hotel reservations provisionally for three nights.'

'Oh, Jordan...'

As she saw the expression of gratitude and affection on her mother's face, Tamsin spun away. How could her intelligent, astute mother be so gullible as to be duped by Jordan? It was easy to wave a magic wand and play shining white knight when you had a company jet and hordes of minions at your disposal awaiting your every order. But she noted that Jordan wasn't planning to accompany her mother, wasn't exactly rushing to his father's bedside himself. No. It simply eased his conscience to send her mother in his stead.

Stop it, she chided herself with sudden self-disgust. What did Jordan's motivation matter? What did it matter if she'd wanted to be the one to wave the magic wand? The important thing was that her mother would shortly be on her way to Andrew, travelling in first-class luxury.

She was suddenly conscious of Jordan's eyes on her face, had the uncomfortable sensation that yet again he had guessed her thoughts and was amused by them. Did nothing ever prick, let alone shake that arrogant self-esteem?

'I'd better go and change. Pack a case...' Her mother rose to her feet and then paused, rubbing a hand over her forehead. 'Oh heavens, the removal men...there's still so much to do...we haven't even started on the loft—'

'Mum,' Tamsin intervened swiftly, 'I can—' She snapped her mouth shut, her eyes clouding with intense irritation as the deep, assured voice overrode hers.

'Don't worry about anything, Anne. I'm sure Tamsin and I can manage.' Jordan leaned back against the door jamb and quirked a dark eyebrow in her direction. 'Can't we, Tammy?' he enquired smoothly.

'Of course we can,' she returned with a dazzling smile. Like hell! Tammy... No one had used that particular diminutive of her name since she'd been about six. She would play along with this for now for her mother's sake, but if Jordan seriously thought for one moment that she wanted or would accept assistance from him, would willingly endure a second longer in his obnoxious presence than was strictly necessary...

'Come on, Anne, or we'll miss the slot,' Jordan murmured softly.

For a second, her mother didn't move, her gaze focused on the towering, lean figure, and then she smiled. 'Thank you, Jordan,' she said quietly.

Laying a hand on her shoulder, he propelled her gently into the hall, and for an imperceptible second, Tamsin witnessed the unguarded expression on his face, saw the deep respect and affection in his eyes as they rested on the slight, fair-headed woman. Her stomach muscles clenched. Jordan had never looked at her like that....

She watched under her lashes as he removed his jacket, revealing a blue cashmere sweater, and tossed it casually over the back of a chair. Swinging away, she switched the kettle back on and mechanically began slicing bread.

There had been an instant rapport between her mother and Jordan from the start, some intangible bond. That year he'd disappeared to the States, he'd corresponded regularly with her mother, telephoned her... and she hadn't received as much as a postcard.

Unseeingly, she stared out of the window into the garden, vividly recalling the times she'd discovered Jordan ensconced in the kitchen, chatting idly with her mother as he sampled her home-made fruit cake with schoolboy relish. There had been an expression of complete tranquility on his face on those occasions that she'd never witnessed before or since. An expression that had always evaporated the moment she'd walked through the door.

She flicked a glance over her shoulder. Long legs stretched out in front of him, Jordan was leaning back in a chair, scanning the newspaper that he'd picked up off the table. He was completely oblivious to her presence, had simply switched off her entire existence. In contrast, she registered with a mixture of unease and resentment, try as she might, she found it impossible to block him out. It was as if she had grown unwanted antennae that were tuned in against her will to that male voltage that permeated every corner of the kitchen.

Idly, he crossed one leg over a knee, the movement causing the denims to tighten along the muscular thigh.

Her throat constricting, Tamsin jerked her gaze upwards and her eyes encompassed the sprinkle of fine dark hair revealed at the V of the sweater that was moulded to the deep chest and flat stomach.

She was caught completely off guard as he suddenly raised his head and she had to fight to stop the betraying colour rushing to her face.

'Would you like a sandwich?' she demanded curtly.

'Just a coffee, please,' he drawled lazily.

'Late breakfast?' she enquired sweetly before she could stop herself and regretted it immediately. If he thought for one moment that she was even the slightest bit interested in his private life...

He didn't answer. Stretching up his arms, he folded his hands lazily behind his head and surveyed her with thoughtful dark eyes. Then quite deliberately, his gaze dropped from her face and moved slowly down the length of her body and then up again.

Don't bite, Tamsin ordered herself. Ignore him. Her whole body fired with warmth as she realized that a few seconds earlier she had been guilty of a similar appraisal, her inspection of Jordan just as thorough. Taking a deep, controlling breath, she picked up a coffee mug, placed it wordlessly in front of Jordan and then, armed with a tray, walked out the door.

The moment she moved into the hall, she expelled the air from her lungs, tension easing from her body, and made her way upstairs to her mother's room.

'Cheese sandwich and coffee,' she announced.

Her mother looked up from the open suitcase on her bed and smiled. 'I'm not very hungry,' she murmured but picked up the steaming mug and took a long, grateful sip.

'Want a hand?'

'No, I'm fine, darling. Tell Jordan I'll only be a few more minutes.'

Nodding, Tamsin picked up the unwanted sandwich and retraced her steps, hesitating as she reached the hall, conscious of just how reluctant she was to return to the kitchen and its sole occupant. *So why is it that every time I come anywhere near you, you flee like a terrified mouse?* Her teeth clenched together. She was not frightened of Jordan Keston!

She paused in the open doorway, her eyes drawn like a magnet to the figure still sprawled indolently in the chair. He was completely inert, engrossed in the newspaper, and yet the whole room was charged with latent energy. Slowly, her gaze wandered over the strong, chiselled planes of his face and fell to the firm, straight mouth.

Her throat constricted. She could still feel, taste that taunting mouth against hers, recall with humiliating clarity her own response, knew how close she had come to complete capitulation.

Swallowing hard, she walked silently into the kitchen and switched on the kettle. She was acting like an adolescent with this stupid post-mortem and tortuous recriminations. The whole episode had been meaningless and insignificant. Just forget it, she ordered herself brusquely.

Armed with her mug and sandwich, she advanced toward the table and faltered. Damn it all! She threw a baleful glare at the back of the dark head. This was still her home, albeit not for much longer, and she refused to allow Jordan to make her feel awkward and self-conscious within its walls.

With a casualness she was far from feeling, she pulled out a chair and sat down opposite him.

'Mum's almost ready.'

Without glancing up from the paper, he gave an incoherent grunt in acknowledgement. Tamsin scowled at her plate. Ill-mannered oaf. She bit into the sandwich and flicked Jordan a glance from under her lashes. His expression was closed and shuttered. A granite mask. She was barely a foot away from him and she might as well be on the moon, she registered. Resentfully, her gaze moved over the harsh male features and her stomach muscles cramped involuntarily. She'd never noticed before just how sensual was the curve of his lower lip.

What would it feel like to be caressed, kissed by Jordan with warmth, tenderness, passion? She dismissed the unwanted, disturbing thought fiercely. Jordan was incapable of any of those feelings. He was emotionally barren, incapable of any depth of feeling for anyone, incapable of commitment to anyone. Witness the stream of women that appeared and disappeared in his life. Witness his current lack of real concern for his father. Her brow furrowed. And she had never once heard him mention his mother. She placed the unfinished sandwich back on her plate. Andrew had been widowed for twenty years, which meant Jordan must have been about fifteen when his mother died. Her eyes darkened reflectively. She knew virtually nothing about his early life, had never once heard him refer to the past.... Her eyes cleared. She wasn't interested in Jordan's past, present or future!

Abruptly, he folded up the newspaper and, leaning back in his chair, surveyed her with fathomless dark blue eyes. Cupping her fingers around her mug, Tamsin met his gaze squarely.

'I wonder if Andrew will have recuperated in time for the wedding,' she murmured casually, taking a nonchalant sip of coffee.

'Hoping for a postponement?' he drawled.

She frowned, confused by the ice in his eyes. 'No, of course not... I just wondered...' Her voice tailed off.

'And it would be just that, Tamsin. A postponement not a cancellation.'

The harshness in the grating voice made Tamsin jolt, her eyes clouding with increasing bewilderment as she saw the condemnation etched on his face.

'You've been opposed to this marriage from the start, haven't you, Tamsin? A fact you've made abundantly clear to both Andrew and your mother. The night they announced their engagement you hardly spoke, sat there sulking like a spoilt, selfish brat.'

'I was tired that night, that's all,' she flared defensively but couldn't stop the wash of colour flooding her face. 'I'd been on early shift for seven days on the trot.'

She looked down at her plate, vividly recalling that celebratory dinner at the West End restaurant. She'd guessed the reason for the dinner invitation long before Andrew and her mother had broken the news, had also anticipated that Jordan would be present for the occasion.

But she'd expected him to come alone, hadn't expected him to arrive with a willowy brunette clinging to his arm. The brunette had monopolized Jordan the entire evening, Tamsin remembered, and in an alcohol-induced exchange of girlish confidences in the powder-room had coyly informed her that she and Jordan would shortly be making a similar announcement.

Tamsin's mouth curved. That announcement had failed to materialize. In fact, the next time she'd seen Jordan he'd been accompanied by a vivacious redhead.

She glanced up, her hackles rising as she saw the expression of contempt on Jordan's face. She'd had enough of this! If he wanted the truth, he could have it.

'I'm glad that my mother is happy but obviously I would have preferred her to be happy with my father,' she admitted brusquely. 'Is that a crime?'

'It's time you grew up and faced facts, Tamsin. Stopped blaming your mother for the failure of your parents' marriage. Stopped kidding yourself that their separation was a slight misunderstanding, and had Andrew not appeared on the scene, they would have eventually walked hand in hand into the sunset.'

Tamsin's mouth tightened at the derision in his voice. The man had as much sensitivity, as much compassion as a brick wall. Didn't he have the wit to appreciate just how painful this still was for her? She wished she'd never asked that innocuous question about Andrew's recovery, should have known that it was impossible to have a normal, civilized conversation with Jordan. He had to turn everything into a battle.

'My mother was the one who instigated the divorce proceedings,' she muttered shortly.

'And do you know why?' he enquired softly.

Tamsin's eyes darkened uneasily. She had the uncomfortable feeling that she was heading into a trap. 'I hardly think it is any of your business,' she snapped. Why couldn't he just let the subject drop?

'Your father was consistently unfaithful to your mother throughout their married life. As you damn well

know. Except you are too much of a coward to face up
to it.'

For a second, Tamsin felt as if she had stopped
breathing, shocked rigid by the brutality in the deep
voice. 'I don't believe it... you're lying—'

'Your mother endured years of humiliation and pain,'
Jordan continued ruthlessly. 'And do you know why?
Because of you. Because she wanted to protect you,
didn't want to shatter your illusions. And now she's
finally found the happiness she deserves, you're doing
your damnedest to spoil it for her with your silent accusations and priggish judgements.'

'No!' She wasn't going to listen to any more of this.
Scraping back her chair with all her force, her face ashen,
Tamsin sped into the hall, dived into the cloakroom on
the left and slammed the door behind her.

Leaning back against it, she began to shudder, trying
desperately hard to deny the memories that unfurled re-
lentlessly in her head. Her mother's white face and red-
rimmed eyes explained away by 'head colds' and
'migraines'. Her father's absences at the dinner table explained away by late-night business meetings. The raised
voices that were instantly hushed when she walked into
the room...

No! She refused to believe it. Her adored father... he
wouldn't do that to her mother...to her. This was simply
one of Jordan's sadistic jokes. How could anyone be so
cruel, so callous? God, she hated Jordan with every fibre
of her being... hated him all the more because she knew
he had only told her the truth.

Dull-eyed, she switched on the taps in the porcelain
basin and splashed cool water onto her burning face.
Jordan, she thought drearily, had been right. She'd

known for years that her parents' marriage had been a sham, that they'd been playing happy families solely for her benefit. And even now they were prolonging the farce, pretending that the divorce was completely amicable, that they were still friends. And she had gone along with the game, blocking her mind to reality because it was easier, much more preferable than facing the truth.

How had Jordan known about her father? Had her mother confided in him? Raising her head slowly, she stared in the mirror above the basin and jolted with revulsion as she saw her bruised, swollen mouth. Teeth gritted together, she reached for the bar of soap and scrubbed her face unmercifully, wishing desperately it was as simple to wash Jordan himself out of her life forever.

She froze as he heard the tap at the door, the sound of her name. 'Go away, damn you,' she muttered ferociously under her breath, dabbing her face with a towel.

'Tamsin?' The tapping grew more insistent. For a moment, she didn't move, and then on legs that felt like jelly crossed the tiled floor and flung the door open.

'Yes?'

Hands raised in front of him as if warding off an attack, Jordan towered over her. 'I'm sorry,' he said quietly.

Tamsin surveyed him in stony silence. And that made everything all right, did it? She slammed the door in his face and had the brief satisfaction of hearing his muffled oath before his footsteps retreated down the hall.

She'd always known that Jordan returned her antipathy but hadn't realized until today the intensity of his dislike, the strength of his aversion to her. It wasn't his revelation about her father that had so shocked her, she acknowledged slowly, but his motivation in doing so. He had wanted to hurt her, deliberately set out to do it, using any ammunition within his grasp, regardless of how cruel. Her mouth tightened. One insincere, glib apology didn't change anything. Unconsciously, her fingers twisted through the towel still clutched in her hands.

The sound of her mother's voice echoing down the hall brought her sharply back to the present. Tossing the towel back over the basin rail, she took a deep breath, squared her small chin resolutely and emerged from the cloakroom.

'Oh, there you are, darling,' her mother greeted her, standing at the foot of the stairs buttoning up her coat. 'I'm just off,' she added rather unnecessarily.

Through the open front door, Tamsin could see Jordan stowing a small suitcase into the boot of the silver grey sports car.

'Give my love to Andrew,' she said awkwardly. There was so much she wanted to say.... Unceremoniously, she threw her arms around her mother and hugged her, realizing with shooting shame that it had been a long time since she'd been so demonstrative. Perhaps now, she thought with a surge of hope, that unspoken barrier between them would start to crumble.

Standing on the front doorstep, she watched as Jordan opened the car door for her mother, his expression gentle, his stance oddly protective as he loomed over her. Closing the door, he moved round to the driver's side and then paused, looking over the car roof at Tamsin.

The warmth and gentleness had been erased from his face. It was now a cold, unresponsive mask.

'Don't start on the loft until I get back,' he said curtly. 'Finish off in the lounge first.'

Tamsin looked back at him incredulously, out of deference to her mother swallowing back her instinctive retort. He just couldn't resist it, could he? Even now, he couldn't resist trying to wind her up, barking out orders at her.

As the car disappeared down the drive, she turned back into the house, feeling the instant sense of relief she always experienced after escaping Jordan's presence. She could never relax with him, was always on guard waiting for his sniping taunts. He sapped her of all energy, left her mentally and physically drained.

She shook her head with disbelief. To think that there had actually been a time when she'd deliberately sought out Jordan's company. She could feel the hysterical bubble of laughter rising in her throat. To think that there had been a time when she'd actually been insane enough to imagine that she was in love with him....

CHAPTER THREE

THE bubble of laughter died in Tamsin's throat. Slowly, she walked across the hall and sat down on the bottom step of the stairs. Drawing up her legs, she clasped her hands around her knees.

Of course she hadn't really been in love with Jordan. She'd been dazzled by him, that's all, too naïve and immature to see beyond the superficial veneer.

Her eyes darkened. It was as if she'd been drugged that first summer. Intoxicated by Jordan. He'd dominated her every waking thought, disturbed her sleep. She grimaced with despair for her nineteen-year-old self. She'd been such a prize idiot. For those few short summer months, her whole life had revolved around Jordan, and she existed only for the precious hours she spent with him at Swallow Lodge.

Don't you think it's time to forgive me? For not taking a frustrated nineteen-year-old virgin to my bed ... She cringed with revulsion, instantly denying the veracity of the words. She had romanticized about Jordan, idolized him. It had been little more than a ridiculous, immature schoolgirl crush. She'd been content just to be near him, hear his voice. ...

Oh, come off it, Tamsin, she berated herself fiercely. Be honest, at least with yourself. How many nights had she lain awake, unable to sleep because of that restless, yearning ache inside her? How many times had she longed to touch Jordan, to reach out a tentative hand

and caress the bronzed silky skin of his back as he lay stretched out by the swimming pool?

Hell's bells, she thought with self-disgust, she'd been like a voyeur that summer with her surreptitious visual exploration of Jordan's body. She'd been fascinated by the firm, straight mouth, the lean, strong hands... and always there had been that gnawing frustration that Jordan never seemed to see her as a woman, persisted in treating her as an entertaining kid sister.

She closed her eyes, wincing. At least she had thought her humiliating secret was safe, but all the time Jordan had been fully aware of that turbulence inside her....

She flicked her eyes open. *Every time I turned round, you were there*. He hadn't even liked her. She'd deluded herself into thinking that he at least enjoyed her company, that she amused him, and all the time he'd merely been tolerating her for her mother's sake. He hadn't even cared enough about her to say goodbye before he departed for America.

She could still remember the intensity of that pain, the grey, dreary mist that had engulfed her for months. Blaming Jordan indirectly for the breakup of her parents' marriage had been a shield behind which to hide her hurt. She jerked herself to her feet, her hands tightening on the banisters.

She'd never resented her mother's blossoming romance with Andrew. It had been her mother's affinity with Jordan that she'd truly resented, she admitted, eyes darkening with self-disgust. She'd been jealous of Jordan's preference for her mother's company, his undisguised respect and affection for her, of the old-fashioned, protective courtesy with which he'd always treated her.

Mechanically, Tamsin began to climb the stairs. Oh, God, what a little fool she'd been at nineteen. What a priggish little hypocrite, refusing to accept that all she'd really felt for Jordan was physical attraction. Unable to view it in such basic terms, she'd made it more palatable by convincing herself that she had fallen in love with him.

She started to grin. All that suffering for nothing. Thank heavens it was all over with now. Thank heavens that she could now view Jordan with complete detached objectivity, that there was nothing he could do or say to ever hurt her again. Maybe there were times when she still felt the force of his attraction, when her hormones weren't quite as governable as she would have wished, but she was no longer an immature nineteen-year-old. Emotionally, she was completely secure, able to see Jordan for what he really was. A man of ice. Shallow, cold, motivated only by a thirst for power. And that man repelled her.

She was stuck. Well and truly stuck. Squashing the stirring of panic, Tamsin cursed herself resoundingly for her stupidity.

The child's cot hadn't seemed particularly heavy when she'd pushed it across the dusty floor, but now, with one end perched precariously on the edge of the loft opening and the other end balanced on her shoulders, it weighed a ton. She didn't have the strength to push it back up, nor the strength to take its complete weight if she moved another step down the ladder. And her arms and shoulders ached excruciatingly, threatened to give way completely, the result of which didn't bear contemplation. Her eyes flickered over the landing banisters, down the curve of the stairwell to the hard, tiled floor below. She shuddered convulsively, forcing her gaze back upwards.

She couldn't stay like this much longer. Had to do something. Somehow had to push the cot back into the loft. Gritting her teeth, she summonsed every ounce of strength and stretched up.

'What the hell do you think you're playing at?'

The curt voice startled her, her hold on the cot lessened, and eyes widening with horror, she felt herself overbalancing, slipping backwards, the cot descending on her like a steam roller.

The yelp of alarm suffocated in her throat as she cannoned backwards into an impenetrable wall. A wall made of hard, rock-solid muscles. Jordan was pinning her forwards against the ladder, holding her immobile as he eased the weight of the cot from her arms.

'You're quite safe now, Tam. Take it easy.'

She gulped for breath, legs and arms feeling like jelly, as the quiet, authoritative voice spoke in her ear. Safe. She wasn't going to be crushed beneath the cot, fall like a rag doll to the treacherously hard floor below.

'Feel steadier?' Jordan enquired calmly.

She nodded. She could feel the warmth of his hard, lean body seeping through her sweatshirt, feel the warmth of his breath on the nape of her neck.

'Fine,' she croaked. Every part of her was being enveloped, suffused by Jordan.

'Right. Move down to the next rung. That's it ... next one ... steady ... one more. Now see if you can slither under my arms.'

With a sigh of relief, Tamsin felt the landing carpet beneath her feet and moved aside quickly to allow Jordan more room for his own descent. He'd changed into a faded denim shirt, the sleeves of which were rolled back on his arms. Tamsin watched as with seemingly effortless ease he slowly lowered the cot to the floor, the hard band of muscle in his shoulders clearly defined beneath his shirt, the sinews of his tanned forearms pronounced.

'Thank you,' she said casually as he straightened up. 'It was a little heavier than I thought,' she continued airily and faltered as she saw the expression on his face. He looked as if he was going to explode, wanted to pick her up and shake her like a rat.

'Of all the damn fool stupid...what the hell did you think you were doing?'

Tamsin's chin jerked up. She didn't need this. 'I was managing perfectly well until you startled me,' she lied forcefully.

'You could have been seriously injured!'

Tamsin looked up into the blazing blue eyes. She'd never seen Jordan display such intensity of emotion, not even anger. He was normally so controlled, so completely in command of himself. Warmth spurted through her. His anger was ignited by concern for her, concern that she could have been hurt....

'Your mother has enough on her plate right now without worrying about your landing up in hospital with a broken leg.'

Tamsin was conscious of the appalling sense of deflation. It was her mother he was concerned for, not her, and doubtlessly the inconvenience to himself if he'd had to cart her off to hospital.

'I told you not to start on the loft until I returned.'

Her chin squared. 'And who the hell do you think you are giving me orders? I'm not in your employ yet!'

Her eyes blazed back into the blue ones, and to her disbelief she saw Jordan's lips twitch, the straight mouth beginning to quirk upwards.

'Did you know you've a cobweb in your hair?' he enquired conversationally, 'And a dirty great smudge down your left cheek?'

And that was funny? She gave him a withering glance, perversely refusing to wipe her cheek, nonplussed by his rapid change of mood.

'Come on, Tarzan. Lift up your end and we'll put this out of the way in a bedroom.'

Shrugging, she did as she was bid, fighting back the sudden burst of inane giggles welling in her throat at the sheer incongruity of the situation. She and Jordan manoeuvring a baby's cot into a spare room like prospective parents...

The giggle died in her throat, the scenario no longer funny but oddly disturbing. She flicked a glance upwards at Jordan as he backed down the landing. His expression was completely impassive, his eyes dark and shuttered as they rested on the cot.

Had marriage, a family, ever been on his agenda? Her eyes explored his face and admitted defeat. It was impossible even to guess at what was going on in that dark head. She pursed her lips. Even her vivid imagination couldn't conjure up the image of Jordan as loving husband and doting father.

He would regard a wife as yet another of his acquisitions, someone to manipulate, bend to his will, the bearer of his son and heir. Doubtlessly, he would give his family every material advantage but he would never give a hundred per cent of himself. His family would be little more than another subsidiary in his empire, would remain on the periphery of his life; it would never form his whole life....

'So you've decided to accept the job with Lyne Air?'

She was lost in thought so it took a second for the drawling words to penetrate Tamsin's head. She had forgotten her earlier remark. Unenthusiastically, she surveyed Jordan across the cot, wishing with all her heart she could tell him that she'd had a better offer.

'It'll do as a stopgap for now,' she said finally and to her intense irritation saw the blue eyes gleam. He was laughing at her, knew just how much it was costing her to accept his job. Her hands tightened around the edge of the cot as Jordan pushed open the door at the end of the landing with a shoulder. She wasn't going to mention the interview, wouldn't give him the satisfaction. As her eyes flickered over the strong, assured face, she felt the familiar surge of antagonism scalding through her. He was always so much in control, so damn sure of himself.

'Why the hell did you offer me the job of senior duty officer if you'd no intention of really giving it to me?'

When she released her hold on the cot, her end crashed to the floor, knocking her shin-bone. With a yelp of pain, Tamsin hopped over to the window-seat, rubbing her ankle.

'I think you must be under some misapprehension.' Jordan surveyed her blandly. 'I didn't offer you the position of S.D.O. I merely informed you that such a vacancy existed at Lyne Air and that you might be interested in applying.' He raised a dark eyebrow. 'Sorry, I didn't quite catch that.'

'Nothing,' Tamsin ground through clenched teeth.

'Oh, I see,' Jordan murmured thoughtfully. 'You were under the impression that you merely had to make a guest appearance at Lyne Air and I would hand you the position of S.D.O. on a plate.' His eyes glinted. 'Tsk, tsk, Tamsin, you don't think I'd stoop to nepotism, do you? Sacrifice my integrity on your account?'

Very droll. Tamsin glowered at her grazed ankle. Jordan would stoop to whatever he chose if it so suited his purposes. He was completely unprincipled, would never be influenced or dictated to by social mores or conventions. That was what made him so completely invincible. He was unaffected by other people's opinions, answerable only to himself.

'You prejudged me before the interview . . . had no intention—'

'I admit I had reservations about your lack of experience—'

'I was . . . am . . . perfectly capable—'

'But I was prepared to give you a chance at the interview to convince me to the contrary,' Jordan continued smoothly, ignoring her interruption. 'Which you failed abysmally to do.'

'That interview was a complete farce from start to finish!'

'I agree. And if it was an example of your standard performance, I'm not damn well surprised you're currently unemployed. Scowling and grunting monosyllabically at the floor is not a technique designed to impress prospective employers. In fact, if it hadn't been for your references, we wouldn't have risked offering you even a temporary position.'

'You checked my references?' Tamsin echoed incredulously. She was prepared to admit that she hadn't exactly covered herself in glory at the ill-fated interview and that Jordan might—just might—conceivably have some justification for his criticism, but he had been acquainted with her for four years, would shortly be related to her by marriage. Couldn't he take anything or anyone on trust?

Slowly, she rose to her feet and followed Jordan from the room, wondering why she felt so absurdly betrayed. *We*? She frowned. 'Who's Sara Lyne?' she asked with studied casualness, her eyes fixed on the back of the dark head.

'A major shareholder in Lyne Air and one of your future employers,' he returned drily, turning to face her as he reached the ladder. 'Her father founded the company, and when he died a year ago, Sara inherited his holding.'

Tamsin wrinkled her nose. She'd guessed the name was too great a coincidence and was startled by how much she resented the fact that the other woman must have discussed her with Jordan.

Whistling under his breath, Jordan repositioned the ladder beneath the loft.

'We used to live together.'

The casually tossed words were so totally unexpected, so totally out of character that for a second Tamsin wondered if she'd heard correctly. Sara Lyne and Jordan...live-in lovers. She felt as if she'd been kicked in the stomach.

'Kiss-and-tell time, Jordan?' she enquired acidly. 'Save it for the tabloids.' Sara Lyne and Jordan... They'd shared not just a bed, but a home, their lives. How long had the relationship lasted? Who had terminated it? The questions hammered in her head, but she refused to voice them, refused to walk into the baited trap and give him the opportunity to snub her.

'So that's why you're backing Lyne Air? For old times' sake?' She smiled at him sweetly. 'Letting sentiment influence your business judgement?'

He smiled back at her blandly. 'Right, up you go, Tamsin.'

She might have guessed that it would be impossible to goad him into an indiscretion. Mechanically, Tamsin moved towards the ladder and began climbing up, belatedly registering just how instinctive it had been, yet again, to instantly obey Jordan's command. Irritated with herself, she paused, flicking a glance downwards over her shoulder.

Jordan, one foot resting on the bottom rung, was quite blatantly studying the firm, rounded curve of her jean-clad hips and bottom with undisguised masculine interest. Damn voyeur. Tamsin's eyes darkened with immediate disdain, furiously aware of the tingling, teasing warmth curdling in the pit of her stomach. He was appraising her as if she were an exhibit in a cattle market and her body was actually responding, she thought with incredulous self-disgust.

As he lifted his gaze and encompassed her frigid expression, his mouth quirked in a slow, unrepentant grin. It would take a hundred-ton steamroller to squash Jordan Keston, Tamsin thought sourly, realizing to her chagrin that she was flushing. Jerking her gaze back upwards, she clambered swiftly into the loft. Without waiting for Jordan to join her, determined to concentrate solely on the task in hand, she padded across the dusty floorboards and started to inspect the contents of two large trunks stowed in the far corner.

She hadn't realized that it was so late. As she replaced the telephone receiver back on the hook, Tamsin looked out of the hall window into the gathering dusk, her mouth curving as she saw Jordan emerge from the garage, a black refuse bag tossed carelessly over his broad shoulder. Hair tousled, shirt dishevelled, jeans as dusty as her own, he looked almost human.

She couldn't have managed without him this afternoon, Tamsin admitted honestly, her eyes following the lean figure as he moved with long, fluid strides down the drive and deposited the refuse bag with the rest of the rubbish awaiting collection. She had expected him to depart after they'd finished in the loft, but to her surprise he'd remained, helping her clear out the outhouses and garage. She grinned. Perhaps, accustomed to being sheltered from the mundane chores of life by a bevy of willing domestic staff, he'd enjoyed the novelty of it.

And neither had their enforced proximity proved to be as much of an ordeal as she'd anticipated. It was as if he'd miraculously undergone some personality change since first entering the house that morning, the man with the taunting eyes and caustic comments transformed into an easygoing, good-humoured companion.

She'd been cautious, wary of him at first, like a mouse with a suddenly reformed feline, waiting for him to pounce, but slowly she'd begun to relax. Her grin broadened, her eyes softening into golden pools. She'd even been persuaded by his plaintive demand for chocolate biscuits mid-afternoon to rush down to the local shop and buy a packet of his favourite brand.

Humming under her breath, Tamsin walked down the hall into the kitchen and glanced up at the clock. Five hours of Jordan's undiluted company and they hadn't even bickered. That must deserve an entry in the record book.

After washing her hands in the sink, she rifled one of the packing cases and removed the first-aid kit. Sitting down at the table, she extracted a sterilized needle and examined the index finger of her right hand.

'Splinter?'

Tamsin glanced up as Jordan appeared through the back door and smiled. 'Mmm.' She couldn't remember the last time she had felt so unconstrained, at ease in his presence. 'Mum just phoned,' she added. 'She's just arrived at the hospital and seen Andrew and all's well.' She summarized the brief exchange.

Jordan nodded but made no comment, moving across to the sink to wash his own hands, and Tamsin was caught totally off guard by the swell of aching emptiness that suddenly and for no logical reason engulfed her. For a few short hours, she and Jordan hadn't been at each other's throats, but nothing had fundamentally changed. There would always be a barrier between them, superficially broken at times, but never completely removed.

Her eyes flickered across the broad, indomitable shoulders. Had Jordan ever been really close to anyone? Had any woman been not just an appendage to his life, but a necessity? Her stomach knotted. Sara Lyne...? She cursed as her hand jerked and the needle dug into her finger.

'Cut that out!' Jordan intervened, forcefully swinging round from the sink.

'What?' Tamsin almost gaped in disbelief at the censorious tone in his voice, the grim disapproval on his face.

'I dislike hearing women swear. It's unfeminine and unattractive. And a habit you seem to have increasingly adopted.'

Tamsin's eyes sparked. 'Of all the pompous, sanctimonious prigs!' Considering his own choice epithets when he'd stubbed his toe earlier on... 'What century are you living in, Jordan?' She snapped her mouth shut as she saw the glint in his eyes. He was winding her up and she'd walked straight into the baited trap, all guns blazing, as usual. Why did she always lose her sense of humour when she was with Jordan? Always overreact to everything he said and did?

'Come on, give me your hand.' Drawing up a chair, Jordan sat down beside her.

She ignored him and continued unsuccessfully with her awkward, left-handed ministrations.

'You'll get frown lines if you scowl like that,' Jordan observed pleasantly and reaching out took hold of her right hand. 'Needle?'

Wordlessly, she handed it to him and stared resolutely ahead, trying to block out the feel of the lean, supple fingers curving around her palm, fighting to ignore the warmth shooting up her arm, spreading slowly and languorously through her body. It took every ounce of concentration to stop her eyelashes flickering downwards, not to lose herself completely in the soporific yet tantalizing sensations flooding over her. She hardly felt the tiny stab of pain as he deftly and gently wielded the needle.

'There,' he murmured with satisfaction as he extracted the splinter.

'Thank you,' she managed to force the word out. Even her scalp was tingling, she realized with appalled horror and her pulse rate seemed to have doubled.

She began to ease her hand from his grasp but his grip tightened. Eyes focused on her face, he slowly and deliberately raised her hand to his mouth and touched the tip of her finger with his lips.

Ye gods! Summonsing every ounce of composure, Tamsin met his gaze squarely. 'Could you pass me a plaster?' she said evenly. Why the hell did he have to keep playing this ridiculous, one-sided game with her? she wondered savagely. What was he trying to prove?

'Would you like me to put it on or can you manage?' he murmured solicitously as he did as she requested. She saw the amused awareness in his eyes and froze inside. You arrogant, self-satisfied bastard. How could she, even for a few short hours that afternoon, have actually liked him? Her stomach suddenly rumbled, the sound seemingly deafening in the silent kitchen, making her conscious of just how long it had been since her half-eaten sandwich.

'Hungry?' Jordan enquired idly, stretching his arms above his head, the movement causing the denim shirt to tauten across the deep chest and powerful shoulders. Scraping back his chair, he rose unhurriedly to his feet and glanced at his gold wristwatch. 'I'll make a reservation at Andre's for eight-thirty.' He moved towards the door. 'That should give us both time to shower and change.'

Before Tamsin had time to gather her startled wits, he had disappeared into the hall. He had to be joking! She heard the front door slam close. This was simply another of his perverse games. Jumping to her feet, she darted out of the kitchen door and sped round the side of the house. He hadn't even had the courtesy to ask her. He'd evidently assumed with his customary high-handed arrogance that no woman could possibly refuse him, would even consider passing on the chance of an intimate dinner at an exclusive restaurant with the great Jordan Keston.

'Jordan!'

In the process of unlocking his car, he acknowledged her approach with a casual wave of his hand but didn't pause. She ground to an abrupt halt. Did he think that she'd come rushing out of the house merely to bid him a fond farewell? Damn it, she wasn't going to go racing down the drive to catch him up! Inserting two fingers in her mouth, Tamsin let out an ear-piercing whistle.

'Good God!'

She had the minor satisfaction of seeing the genuine astonishment on Jordan's face as he spun round away from the car to face her. It had taken her two years and a lot of coaching from one of her male flatmates to perfect that little accomplishment.

'Referee football matches in your spare time?' he enquired as she reached him.

She ignored his comment as unworthy of a reply. Tilting her head, she looked up at him with steady hazel eyes. 'No,' she said flatly and without preamble.

He raised a quizzical eyebrow and then smiled lazily. 'I'll pick you up in an hour.'

Tamsin looked at him in disbelief. What did it take to snub this man? 'I don't want to have dinner with you tonight,' she enunciated slowly and clearly.

He surveyed her thoughtfully for a second. 'Why not, Tamsin?'

Didn't he understand plain English? 'Because I have no desire to spend the evening in your company.' Was that blunt enough? 'Because you're...' The words died in her throat, her stomach dipping without warning as the blue eyes sought and held hers.

'Why not, Tamsin?' he repeated softly, and in the dark navy depths she read the open, unmistakable challenge. Giving her no time to reply, he folded his muscular frame into the driver's seat and the powerful car purred into life.

Tamsin watched it disappear down the drive and then, turning, walked mechanically back into the house, instantly aware of the silence, the emptiness. Her eyes alighted on the familiar leather jacket strewn on the floor where it had evidently fallen from the peg. She stooped to retrieve it and then impulsively slipped it over her shoulders, performing a graceful pirouette. Mmm. Not really her style. It dwarfed her completely. She could feel Jordan, smell him....

Glancing self-consciously over her shoulder, she whipped off the jacket and replaced it on the hook. She'd drop it off at Swallow Lodge tomorrow. She grinned. Or take it to a charity shop. Her grin faded abruptly, tiny goose bumps creeping down her spine as she recalled that unspoken challenge in Jordan's eyes.

Padding barefoot across her bedroom, Tamsin surveyed the sparse contents of the wardrobe. It was a toss-up between a clean pair of jeans and sweatshirt or the russet jersey dress that she'd only packed as an afterthought in her weekend case. Squashing that perverseness that tempted her to elect for the former, knowing she would only regret it later, she removed the dress and slipped it over her head, flicking the silky curtain of freshly washed hair back over her shoulder.

Head on one side, she inspected herself in the full-length mirror on the wardrobe door. Simple would be the most accurate description of the straight, V-necked dress, she decided thoughtfully. Not simple as in deceptively simple, reeking of an expensive designer tag; simple as in unadventurous, safe.

Unadorned by jewellery, devoid of make-up—her small collection of both were back at her flat—her clear, honey-toned skin flushed pink from the shower, the tiny sprinkle of freckles on her straight nose pronounced, she looked like a fresh-faced, well-scrubbed schoolgirl. She pulled a face. Not exactly a poised, sophisticated woman of the world. More the archetypal girl next door. She grinned. Which, strictly speaking, in Jordan's case was true.

For a second, she wished with all her heart she had something chic, something sexy to wear, something that would make Jordan do a double take, and then dismissed the idea as absurd. Sitting down on the edge of the bed, she slipped on her low-heeled court shoes. Why was she going tonight? She still had time to change her mind...for about the sixtieth time in as many minutes.

She lifted her head and stared into the mirror, registering the high colour in her cheeks, the glow in her large hazel eyes. Why was she really going tonight? a small voice demanded again. She squared her chin resolutely.

To prove something to herself. To prove that the spark of physical attraction for Jordan was controllable, to reassure herself that her reaction to him today had been no more than a temporary aberration.

She looked at the girl with the grave, over-earnest expression and burst into mocking laughter. Rats to that. Spare the psychology. She was going out tonight with Jordan because she wanted to. Because whatever her reservations about him, she felt more alive in his company than with any other living person.

She barely had time to absorb this uncomfortable insight when she heard the doorbell chime. She didn't move, her whole body frozen into inaction. The bell rang again, more insistently, and adrenalin spurted through her in frenetic waves, releasing her from her paralysis.

Grabbing her handbag, she gave her bedroom a swift, backward glance and, curbing her instinct to rush, made her way slowly and sedately down the stairs.

The bell pealed again, echoing stridently through the house.

'All right, I'm coming!' She flung open the door, her exasperation forgotten at the sight of Jordan in a formal, expertly tailored dark suit, a red silk tie nestling against his brilliant white shirt. Her stomach muscles cramped. He looked urbane, sophisticated and overpoweringly masculine.

'I was beginning to think I'd been stood up,' he drawled, his gaze moving over her in a slow, arrogant sweep.

'And you would have been scarred for life,' Tamsin retorted drily, her hackles rising under his appraisal, the expression in his eyes clearly indicating that her appearance was wanting. She doubted whether Jordan knew the meaning of the word 'rejection', had ever been plagued by the insecurities that most mere mortals endured.

'Doesn't bear thinking about,' Jordan agreed solemnly. The straight mouth twitched, the blue eyes turning from navy to azure.

Tamsin's stomach dipped. Swiftly, she turned to slam the front door shut and then picked her way carefully down the gravel path to the sleek car. She gave a small grimace as she looked downwards. Her shoes could have done with a quick polish. Without thinking, she halted and, reverting to her school days, absently rubbed each foot in turn behind the opposite calf. Looking up, she saw the unsuppressed amusement in Jordan's eyes as he stood by the car, holding the passenger door open for her. She flushed scarlet.

'Sweet sixteen,' he murmured. 'I hope you've some ID in your handbag.'

'Yes, and a clean handkerchief,' she returned tartly, 'and I've promised to be home by ten.' She felt anything but sweet, and fourteen would be nearer the mark. Her confidence seemed to be ebbing away by the second.

Slipping into her seat, she stared rigidly ahead, every sense, every inch of her skin aware of Jordan as he joined her.

'Do you realize that this is the first time you and I have been out to dinner together unchaperoned?' Jordan drawled as he turned on the ignition and the car moved smoothly down the drive into the lane.

Tamsin shrugged as if the thought had never once occurred to her, keeping her gaze focused strictly ahead.

'Would you like some music?'

Acquainted with Jordan's tastes in classical music, and aware of her own emotional response to it, she shook her head. She felt vulnerable enough already. In the silent car, she could hear Jordan's light, even breathing, could feel her own chest rising and falling in matching rhythm.

'Was that a yes or a no?'

She gave a noncommittal grunt.

'And who claimed that the art of conversation was dead?' Jordan murmured drily. 'Are you going to spend the entire evening sulking or is it just a quick phase?'

'I'm not sulking,' Tamsin flared. 'Just tired, that's all.' And angry. Angry because she felt so ill at ease, defensive, unsure of herself. Angry with Jordan for making her feel like that and angry with herself for letting him. 'And if you want non-stop inane chatter, buy a parrot.' She jerked her head round towards him. 'Why did you invite me out tonight?' she demanded bluntly, posing the question that had nagged at her from the first. Invite? That was a joke! He'd simply taken her acquiescence for granted.

'Because it's my housekeeper's night off and I hate eating alone,' he returned smoothly.

'How sad.' Poppycock. Jordan was the most self-sufficient person she'd ever met. And neither would he ever want for female companions.

'Why did you accept?' He raised a quizzical eyebrow. 'Other than out of consideration for my fragile male ego.'

Despite herself, Tamsin's mouth curved. 'I was hungry and I make it a policy never to turn down the offer of a free meal,' she said airily.

'Just a sweet, old-fashioned girl, hmmm?' His mouth quirked upwards, revealing strong white teeth, the brilliant blue eyes crinkled at the corners and he threw back his head and roared with laughter.

The rare, rich mellow sound reverberating through the car was too infectious, impossible to resist, and although she didn't have a clue why Jordan found her last remark so amusing, she could do nothing to stop her own bubble of laughter rising in her throat. Perhaps tonight wasn't going to be quite such an ordeal after all.

Tamsin picked up her wineglass from the white damask tablecloth and watched Jordan over the rim as he selected a ripe peach from the bowl in front of him. She had declined a dessert, and Jordan, after a faintly wistful glance at the rich chocolate gateaux on the sweet trolley, had elected to have fresh fruit.

Temporarily unobserved, she allowed her gaze to wander over the strong contours of his assured face, the harsh lines softened in the dim lighting, his eyes shadowed to deep blue pools under the thick black lashes. He lifted his head and smiled.

'Are you sure you won't change your mind and have something?'

She smiled back. 'I couldn't eat another thing,' she confessed and took a swift sip from her glass, glad when Jordan's attention returned to his plate.

She had never felt so completely out of her depth in her entire life. She couldn't cope with this Jordan, this humorous, attentive, considerate stranger, was fighting with every ounce of strength to combat him and that strange, dizzy light-headedness that threatened to engulf her completely, making her take leave of all reason.

She felt as if she were walking towards an abyss—one false step and she would be lost completely. Never before had she been subjected to the full force of Jordan's charm. She could deal with his sarcasm, his caustic comments, retaliate in any verbal battle, but this was something new altogether, a far more potent weapon.

Her eyes flickered around the exclusive, intimate restaurant whose reputation for food was, she'd discovered, amply justified. The room was full of elegant, attractive women—she'd recognized a well-known model—and yet Jordan hadn't given them even a cursory glance, had seemed equally oblivious to the number of feminine eyes that had turned to assess him with undisguised interest. He'd seemed immune to the pretty waitress, treating her with courteous disinterest.

Tamsin swallowed. His whole attention had been focused on her, and her alone. He'd made her feel that she was the most fascinating, enchanting, beautiful woman he'd ever laid eyes on, that her conversation was the most scintillating he'd ever heard. Made her feel as exhilarated as if she had just climbed Mount Everest, as if her blood had turned to champagne....

Her eyes dropped to her glass, her fingers twisting round the stem. It was all an act, a well-practised, well-polished act she reminded herself fiercely ... and she was not going to fall for it as, doubtlessly, countless women had done so before her.

Her eyes flickered across the table, watching with drugged fascination as the juice from the peach trickled down Jordan's lean fingers. Unbidden and unwanted, an image of her mouth and lips tasting the sweetness of the juice and the warmth of Jordan's skin sparked into her head. Her cheeks flamed with colour just as he glanced up.

The blue eyes instantly sought hers, one dark eyebrow raised slightly, and then the well-formed mouth curved. He couldn't possibly know what was going on in her head, Tamsin told herself swiftly but her colour deepened. He was so damned sure of his own masculine attraction, she thought with a stab of bitter resentment. It would never even occur to him that not all women were gullible enough to be bowled over by his fake charm. Well, she wasn't going to be taken in by it, was going to fight every inch of the way.

Jordan dipped the tips of his hands in the finger-bowl and wiped them with the napkin provided.

'Shall we have coffee in the lounge?'

She acquiesced with an easy, casual smile and rose to her feet, instantly aware of Jordan's hand on her elbow as he guided her through the restaurant into the plush lounge beyond and conscious, too, of the number of female heads that turned to view their progress. She glanced sideways up at Jordan and was shaken by the surge of fierce, possessive pride that tore through her, a pride she reminded herself shortly that she had no right to feel. She was slightly appalled and ashamed, also, to acknowledge that she was actually enjoying being the target of so many envious glances.

She needed to get a grip on herself, desperately needed a respite from Jordan to rearm her defences.

'I think I'll just freshen up.' The powder-room to the left loomed like a sanctuary. She felt relieved and yet oddly bereft as Jordan's hand fell to his side, acutely conscious of his eyes following her as she headed away from him across the thick carpet.

The powder-room was deserted, and crossing to the row of marble basins, Tamsin switched on a tap and held her wrist under the cool running water, waiting until she could feel her pulse rate return to normal. Extracting a comb from her bag, she ran it through her silky waves and then stiffened in bemusement as she saw her reflection in the full-length mirror.

It must be a trick of the light... The much-maligned dress, looking nearer gold than reddish brown, picked out the golden glints in her hair. The soft material hinted enticingly at the curves it shielded, flattering her in a way she hadn't thought possible. Her skin glowed with vitality, her eyes under the thick sweep of dark lashes were luminous, mysterious pools.

In the past few hours she seemed to have undergone some miraculous transformation. Far from the awkward, uncertain girl next door, she looked confident, vibrant, sexy, had the indefinable aura of a woman completely secure in her ability to attract and hold male attention.

A cold shudder crawled down her spine. It was Jordan who had been the catalyst, had wrought this metamorphosis. He could reduce her to a gauche teenager, a sullen, inarticulate dolt, could spark her into a spitting virago... and tonight with a few smiles and a pinch of insincere, wordless flattery...

Her small jaw clenched. How could she be so weak as to let him manipulate her like this, influence her so dramatically? To allow her own moods to be so completely dependent on his? Ye gods, she was allowing him to treat her like a mindless lump of putty!

Picking up her handbag, teeth gritted together, she marched out into the lounge. She'd spotted Jordan immediately. The lounge was dimly lit, was wall-to-wall with attractive, successful men and yet it was as if Jordan was sitting in his own personal spotlight.

She was suddenly so angry she wanted to scream and yet she wasn't even a hundred per cent sure why. Jordan had seen her, half-rising to his feet as she approached, a welcoming smile hovering on the straight mouth. It would almost be worth causing a scene just to see his reaction. Her mouth twisted wryly. He would simply deal with it with his usual aplomb and unshakeable assurance. Nothing would ever faze Jordan, she thought bitterly, certainly not a mere hysterical female.

'White. No sugar.' He quirked an eyebrow at her as she sank into the deep, comfortable chair drawn to the low table.

'Thank you,' she said coolly. As she took hold of the proffered cup, his hand brushed hers. Was that deliberate or accidental? The physical contact had been minimal and yet it was as if she'd stuck her hand into an electric socket. Drinking her coffee swiftly, she deliberately turned her head away from Jordan and watched the couples on the dance floor as they moved languorously to the easily recognizable melodies issuing from the small band on the rostrum. Unconsciously, she began to tap her foot in time to the slow rhythm.

'Would you like to dance?' Jordan asked softly.

She wanted to refuse, her stomach dipping at the thought of the inevitable intimacy involved in dancing together. If the band would play something a little faster, less blatantly romantic... Before she had time to voice her disinclination, he reached out a hand and drew her gently to her feet. In vain, she tried to ignore the warm fingers curved around her palm, tried without success to mentally distance herself as his hand dropped to the curve of her waist and he drew her towards him.

She focused her eyes at a point above his shoulder, but it was impossible not to be aware of the square, uncompromising jawline, the tenacious, stubborn chin on a level with her forehead.

The hand on her back increased its pressure, drawing her even closer into the circle of his arms as he guided her skilfully across the floor. She felt his jaw brush the top of her head, could feel the warmth of his body against hers, and her resistance collapsed, her senses beginning to reel.

She was floating off into a rosy haze of unreality. It seemed to be the most natural thing in the world to allow her head to fall on the accommodating hard shoulder, tilting her face up towards his.

She wanted to lift a hand and gently explore the planes of that strong, commanding face, to feel the warm texture of his skin beneath her palm. Her gaze lingered on the firm, straight mouth, barely inches away from hers, and her eyes flickered half-closed. But more than anything in the world, she wanted... Oh, my God! It must be the wine... she wasn't used to it... rarely drank except for the occasional half pint of beer with Tom... oh, no! The rosy bubble exploded in her ears.

'Tom!' She didn't realize that she had spoken his name out loud until she felt Jordan stiffen against her. How could she have simply forgotten Tom? Shame and recrimination tore through her as she came to an abrupt halt. How could she have done that to her closest friend, left him hanging around for hours?

'Tom?' Jordan enquired coolly. His hold on her relaxed, his arms falling to his side.

'I was supposed... we had arranged...' she faltered. She couldn't bring herself to tell him the truth. 'I didn't realize it was so late,' she tried again, forcing a casual lightness into her voice. 'Tom's expecting me back at the flat tonight...he'll be worried....'

'There's a phone in the foyer. Call him and explain where you are.'

Tamsin hesitated, puzzled by the sudden intensity in Jordan's eyes that was at odds with the drawling tone. Then deciding she must have imagined it, she shook her head.

'No.' What did she say if he did pick up the phone, always assuming Tom wasn't in bed or hadn't given up on her and gone out anyway? Sorry for standing you up tonight but I had a better offer and went to Andre's with Jordan? She cringed inwardly. Much better to grovel in person. 'I really ought to be getting back to the flat....'

'I see.'

There was a wealth of meaning in the two terse words but Tamsin didn't even attempt to analyse them, too bewildered by the mask that had slammed down over Jordan's face. Even his eyes seemed to have changed colour to a bleak, forbidding grey. Then before she had time to register what was happening, let alone protest, she found herself being herded off the dance floor and propelled unceremoniously through the tables and chairs to the door.

'I take it we're leaving?' she enquired acidly, shrugging off his hand resentfully as they emerged into the cool night air. So much for urbanity, courtesy, consideration. They were superficial veneers that Jordan donned and shed as easily as he did his shirts. And his fingers had damned well hurt, pressing into the sensitive skin of her upper arm like a steel vice.

'Thug. Ill-mannered lout,' she muttered and shivered.

'Why didn't you bring a jacket with you? Didn't it occur to you that it might be cold when we came out?'

Tamsin glared up at Jordan as they walked towards the car.

'No, it damn well didn't!'

That would have been too sensible. And common sense, rationality, reason, were things that always seemed to be in short supply when she was in his company.

Mechanically, she clambered into the car and sank back in the seat, conscious of her feeling of utter deflation. The past few hours had been a dream. This was normality. Back to the status quo with Jordan.

She groaned silently. What had possessed her to come out to dinner with him? How could she simply have forgotten her prior arrangement with Tom? she berated herself yet again. She frowned with sudden disquiet. She hadn't once thought about Andrew or her mother this evening, either....

Her heart gave a slow, sickening lurch, her throat constricting painfully. She hadn't thought about anyone or anything but Jordan tonight. Because, she thought dully, when she was with him nothing and nobody else in the world existed.

CHAPTER FOUR

IT WASN'T true! Mechanically fastening her seat-belt, Tamsin stared out into the darkness as the car moved off. Her temporary amnesia had been induced by weariness and the unaccustomed wine. Nothing to do with Jordan.

All right. She shrugged mentally. She was prepared to admit that she wasn't completely immune to Jordan but then she wouldn't be female if her hormones didn't recognize and respond in some way to his blatant masculinity. Witness every woman in the restaurant tonight. She may not like him, but it would be impossible not to be aware of him as a man. But that was perfectly normal, well within her control.

Tonight was simply a one-off. And it was hardly surprising that she'd been slightly off keel after the emotional traumas of the day. Packing up her childhood home... Andrew in hospital... the shock of having the truth about her father confirmed. Her chest tightened. That was something she just couldn't think about right now. All in all, it had been a lousy day and the sooner it was over the better.

She wouldn't go back to the flat tonight. Now that she'd had a chance to think more rationally, it would be simpler just to phone Tom from home. Odd how she still thought of it as home.... She suppressed a yawn, exhaustion sweeping over her. All she wanted right now was a long, hot soak in the tub, and then to fall into bed and blank out the past twenty-four hours.

Her eyebrows furrowed together as she suddenly became aware of her surroundings and the direction in which they were heading.

'There's no need to take me all the way back to Croydon,' she protested. 'I don't want to—'

'And how exactly were you planning to get over there yourself at this time of night?'

Jordan's cool, patronizing tone caught her on the raw. 'I was going to borrow Mum's car,' she lied airily, wondering why on earth she didn't simply tell him of her change in plan. But he'd sounded so damn condescending.

'You're in no fit state to drive anywhere. You've had too much to drink,' Jordan informed her brusquely.

Well, she'd certainly walked into that one, Tamsin admitted ruefully and it was a little late to tell him that she'd had no intention of driving anywhere anyway. But he didn't have to sound quite so sanctimonious, so disapproving. She may have had more wine than him but she hadn't exactly finished the evening legless, singing bawdy songs.

This was completely absurd, she thought incredulously as her eyes flicked to the forbidding, shadowy profile. Jordan obviously resented having to make the long detour on her behalf and she didn't even particularly want to go back to Croydon. Why couldn't they communicate about something as simple as this? Why couldn't they ever have an ordinary civilized conversation without it erupting into a battle?

The trouble with Jordan was that he never damn well listened. If he'd let her finish her sentence in the first place, he would have avoided the extra mileage. Well, served him right.

Her eyes moved over the shadowy planes of his face. The harsh male features looked as if they'd been hewn out of granite. He looked tough, uncompromisingly male and as remote as if he were on a separate planet. It was impossible to believe that a short time ago she'd been in his arms....

Damn it all. How dare he simply block her out, act as if she no longer even existed? Just because she'd been the one to initiate the end of the evening instead of him.

'God, you're a selfish bastard,' she exploded. 'Just because you're having to put yourself out for me for once...just because the evening didn't end quite as you'd planned—'

'And how exactly was that, Tamsin?'

'I—' She broke off, registering the dangerous edge to his voice, feeling the quagmire opening beneath her feet.

'Oh, I see.' The moment of reflective silence didn't reassure her one bit. 'You assumed my dinner invitation included breakfast, hmm?'

'What? I—'

'Sorry to disappoint you, Tamsin, but I'm a little fastidious with whom I spend the intervening hours.'

She didn't believe she was hearing this. 'If you imagined for one moment that—'

'Spare me the outraged-innocent routine,' Jordan drawled. 'The invitation's been in your eyes all evening. I could take you to bed any time I choose.' He drew up at a traffic light. 'Except I don't choose.'

Don't explode. Ignore him. You'll never win. The words hammered in Tamsin's head. She didn't know it was possible to hate anybody as much as she did Jordan in that moment. Couldn't bear to be with him a second longer than was necessary. Swiftly unclicking her seatbelt, she reached for the door handle.

'Think about it first,' Jordan advised her conversationally. 'No taxis about. Pitch-dark.' He smiled and then thoughtfully reached across and opened the door for her. 'But it's up to you.'

Face frozen, she swung her legs onto the pavement and hesitated, half in, half out of the car. She didn't have a clue where she was. And as a grand gesture this was fast losing its impact. With as much dignity as she could muster, she scrambled back into the car and closed the door. Head held high, she focused her gaze directly ahead, willing the journey to end.

After what seemed like eternity, Jordan pulled up in front of the converted Victorian house situated at the end of a cul-de-sac. Wordlessly, Tamsin scrambled out and sped up to the front door, keys clutched in her hand. Pausing on the doorstep, she glanced back over her shoulder.

Jordan had made no attempt to follow her, was sitting as motionless as a granite statue. As she entered the house, she heard the sound of the car driving away.

The end to a perfect evening. Closing the front door, she leaned against it for a second. Her anger had dissipated. She felt drained and empty, inexplicably deflated. How had she really expected the evening to end? a small voice suddenly enquired. She dismissed it ruthlessly. She wasn't going to dwell on the evening, analyse everything Jordan had done or said, like some adolescent. She was just going to block it out completely. She took a deep breath. And now, she thought unenthusiastically, she had to pacify Tom.

She'd noticed from outside that the light was on in the communal lounge on the second floor, so presumably he was still up. Her other two flatmates were both away for the weekend. Slowly, she made her way up the stairs, reluctantly passing her bedroom *en route*.

'Tom, I'm so sorry...' she began as she pushed open the lounge door and then faltered at the sight of the fair-headed young man slumped dejectedly on the sofa. 'You lost the match,' she quipped, instantly regretting her facetiousness as she saw the expression on his face.

'I thought something had happened to you,' he said quietly. 'That you'd had an accident.'

'Oh, Tom, I'm sorry,' Tamsin repeated guiltily, moving across the room and sitting beside him. She had half hoped that he would have tired of waiting for her, left a note and spent the evening either commiserating or celebrating with his rugby team-mates. But that patently had not been the case. While she had been dining in an exclusive restaurant, he'd been sitting here worrying.

'You could have at least telephoned,' he said evenly.

'I know. I should have but I just...' Her voice tailed off. What on earth could she say?

'You just forgot,' he completed quietly. 'You spent the evening with Jordan, didn't you? I heard his car driving off.'

She nodded dumbly. Yell at me. Tell me I'm an inconsiderate, thoughtless wretch, that you've wasted the entire evening hanging around for me. But please don't look at me like that, she pleaded inwardly, as she saw the pain in his eyes. He was the last person in the world she would ever want to hurt and this was the last way in which she'd expected him to react to her late arrival, she thought miserably, hating herself. She'd expected him

to be annoyed with her—justifiably so—but had anticipated that he would soon relent, accept her apology and
they would end up having a companionable cup of coffee
together.

'I care a great deal about you, Tamsin.'

Uneasily, she registered both the intensity in his voice
and in his eyes.

'Don't you feel anything for me at all?' he muttered
huskily.

She cleared her throat uncertainly. 'I'm very fond of
you. As a friend.' She didn't want this conversation to
go any further, wanted badly to escape. 'Fancy a coffee?'
she said weakly. She began to rise to her feet.

'No, Tamsin. Please. Just hear me out.' Catching hold
of her hand, he pulled her back down onto the sofa,
turning to face her. 'I want us to be more than just
friends. I wasn't going to say anything just yet...but
I'm so scared once you leave the flat I'll lose you completely.' Raising a hand, he gently tucked an errant lock
of silky hair behind her ear. 'You must know how I feel
about you.'

Tamsin swallowed hard. This couldn't be happening.
She didn't want this to be happening. She saw his head
lower towards her but her reactions were too slow.

For a moment, she remained passive as his lips brushed
against hers. His kiss was warm, tender, and just for one
split second she was tempted to launch herself into the
comforting security of his arms. But it was a decision
she would regret; it wouldn't be fair to Tom.

His mouth increased its pressure, became more
demanding.

'No, Tom...' Raising her hands to his shoulder, she
jerked him away from her and the ensuing un-

comfortable, awkward silence was even worse than she had anticipated.

She couldn't bear to see the mixture of hurt and embarrassment on his face, couldn't bear to draw this out any longer. Jumping to her feet, berating herself for her cowardice, she fled the room and rushed down to her bedroom. Sinking on the bed, she buried her face in her hands. She'd handled the whole situation so badly... if only she'd been more prepared...

The light tap at the door wasn't totally unexpected.

'I'm s-sorry. I wish I hadn't... I've ruined everything now....' There was a pause. 'Can't we forget tonight? Please. Just go back to the way we were?'

The misery in his voice made her heart squeeze. 'Yes,' she agreed quietly, but with a feeling of aching sadness wondered if it would really ever be possible to resume that old, easy friendship. 'Good night, Tom.'

She heard the sound of his footsteps receding and, rising to her feet, began to pace jerkily around the room. Coming to a decision, she went out into the hall and called a twenty-four-hour minicab service. Then while she waited for it to arrive, she changed into a pair of jeans and a sweater and scribbled a quick note for Tom. It would be easier for both of them if she wasn't here in the morning.

Jordan wasn't exactly going to be overjoyed to see her, Tamsin mused gloomily as she mounted the three wide steps to the solid-oak front door. Odds on it would be a grimace and a growled 'What the hell are you doing here?' Well, at least the downstairs lights were still on. She pressed the doorbell, turned to give the cab driver a reassuring smile and nearly jumped out of her skin as she saw a shadowy form appear round the side of the house and come towards her.

'Tamsin.' The familiar drawling voice evinced not the slightest degree of surprise at seeing her, and as he came closer she could see that Jordan had changed from his suit into jeans and a thick blue sweater. Was he in the habit of taking nocturnal rambles around the garden? Tamsin wondered savagely, her heart still pounding from shock.

'Let me guess.' He fished in his pocket for a key and opened the door, light flooding out onto the porch. 'You think you've dropped an earring in the car. It's not worth much in monetary terms but it was left to you by your great-grandmother and is of great sentimental value and you couldn't sleep for fretting about it.'

'Oh, for Pete's sake!' This was all she needed. Had some woman in his past actually used that unoriginal gambit to further an acquaintance with him? She followed him into the house. 'Would you...um...could I...?' Hell, this was even more difficult than she'd imagined. Unconsciously, she glanced back over her shoulder towards the waiting taxi.

'Cash-flow problem?' Jordan murmured sympathetically.

'I've left my purse back in the flat,' she snapped. A fact she'd discovered to her dismay only a short time ago. 'Jordan,' she exclaimed with exasperation as turning on his heel he disappeared into a room on the left.

What did he want? Her to grovel? She was about to dart after him when he reappeared and wordlessly thrust a wad of notes into her hand.

'Thank you,' she muttered ungraciously. 'I'll pay you back tomorrow,' she added coolly and sped outside to the waiting driver, apologizing profusely for the delay. Reeling slightly from the amount of money she'd just handed over, she watched the tail-lights disappear around the bend in the tree-lined drive, turned back to the house and looked at the closed door in disbelief.

Chin squared, she reached for the bell and kept her finger pressed on it until the door opened.

'Still here?' Jordan enquired mildly.

'I need a bed for the night.' She forced the words out through clenched teeth. 'I've left my house keys—'

'Back at the flat with your purse, hmm?'

'As it happens, well, yes,' she admitted and yelped in protest as Jordan's hand closed round her arm. Slamming the door behind him, he propelled her into the large, spacious lounge and pushed her none too gently into a leather armchair. Striding over to the drinks cabinet, he poured a measure of whisky into a glass and swung round to face her.

'Right, Tamsin,' he said smoothly. 'What exactly are you doing here?'

'I've already told you,' she snapped. 'I—'

'Half an hour after I'd dropped you off at the flat, you were suddenly attacked by an overwhelming sentimental desire to spend one last night in your old home. And in your maudlin state you quite inadvertently forgot both your purse and keys.' He raised a sceptical dark eyebrow.

'Oh, go to hell!' And thanks a bunch for the drink. Tamsin's eyes suddenly widened. 'My God, you arrogant, egotistical...you think that this is some devious, subtle feminine plot to—'

'To what, Tamsin?' Eyes gleaming at her sudden discomfort, he tossed the whisky to the back of his throat, poured another measure into the glass and carried it across the room.

'Don't tell me you've forgotten the punch-line?' Sitting back in the armchair drawn up opposite hers, by the red-brick fireplace, he crossed one lean leg over the other and surveyed her with inscrutable dark blue eyes.

'I'd rather sleep in a hedge than under this roof.' Tamsin jumped to her feet. 'It's been a bloody day and I've had enough—'

'Lovers' tiff with Tom, hmm?'

Tamsin froze, slumping back into her chair. How on earth...? 'Tom and I aren't lovers...we're just f-friends.' She regretted the instinctive denial immediately as she saw the glint in the blue eyes.

'But Tom doesn't see it quite like that?' Abruptly, he threw back his head and roared with laughter. 'So the faithful hound has finally shown his teeth. And it all came like a bolt out of the blue. You had absolutely no idea of the way he felt.'

Tamsin's mouth tightened as she looked back at the dark, mocking face, heard the derision in his voice, unhappily aware of the betraying colour flooding her face. Hadn't she had her suspicions about Tom for some time now, alerted by the occasional expression in his eyes, the tone in his voice?

'But you preferred to ignore it. Pretend it wasn't happening because you didn't want it to. You enjoyed having your faithful swain as long as he didn't make any emotional or physical demands on you.'

'That's a revolting thing to say and it's not true!' Tamsin's hands gripped the arms of the chair, her nails sinking into the soft leather.

'Did Tom hurt you in any way tonight? Try and rape you?'

'Of course not! You've got the foulest mind—'

'So why exactly did you feel compelled to run away?' Jordan asked conversationally.

'Because I thought it would be easier, less embarrassing if I wasn't there in the morning,' Tamsin snapped back.

Jordan smiled. 'Easier for whom?' he drawled softly. 'Tom? Or you?'

'I...' she faltered. She broke his gaze and stared down at her hands.

'You're twenty-three years old and you're still living in cloud-cuckoo-land.' The contempt in the grating voice cut through her like a knife. 'Anything unpleasant and you run away, avoid the issue. Your father...Tom...'

'No,' Tamsin muttered, but she could feel the fight draining away from her and realized to her horror that tears were trickling down her face.

'If that's my cue to rush over with tissues and sympathy, forget it, Tamsin.'

Dashing at her face with her hands, Tamsin jerked her gaze to Jordan, registering the complete detachment on his face.

'You're the last person in the world I would expect sympathy, understanding or compassion from. You're like a machine. Devoid of all human emotion.'

Jordan's expression didn't alter. 'Oh, go to bed,' he said dismissively. 'Go and wallow in self-pity in private.'

'You're a bastard, Jordan.' Rising to her feet with as much dignity as she could muster, she walked towards the door. 'And how a courteous, kind, gentle man like Andrew ever fathered a son like you is incomprehensible.'

'Possibly because he didn't. Andrew is my adoptive parent, not my natural father.'

Tamsin whirled back round, wondering if she'd misheard the dry, clipped words, and as she saw the shutters slam down over the blue eyes, the chiselled male features form into a forbidding granite mask, frustration tore through her. She felt like marching over to him and shaking him with all her strength. He did this to her every time. Made some tantalizing personal comment and then shut her out, retreated back into his lair.

'Good night, Jordan. I hope I can reciprocate your warm hospitality one day.'

Slamming the door behind her, Tamsin moved into the hall and slowly made her way up the imposing, carved staircase. Was it common knowledge that Jordan was adopted? Was it only with her that he was so unforthcoming? Her hand tightened on the polished banisters. How could she have not known something as fundamental as that about him? The inexplicable stab of aching emptiness caught her totally unawares, was like a physical pain.

Reaching the top of the stairs, Tamsin surveyed the array of closed doors leading off from the wide, high-ceilinged landing. Presumably, since Jordan hadn't allocated a specific one to her, she had a choice of rooms. Her footsteps silent on the oatmeal carpet, she pushed open a door at random and flicked on the light switch.

Stepping over the threshold, she stopped abruptly, her eyes moving slowly around the room, absorbing the king-size bed, the dark suit hung on the wardrobe door, the white shirt discarded casually over the back of the elegant fireside chair, the assortment of male toiletries on the dressing-table.

It would seem that she had inadvertently stumbled into the lord and master's inner sanctum. And the sooner she beat a hasty retreat the better. Not that she would be the first woman, discounting the housekeeper, to enter this particular domain, she mused acidly. Her eyes flicked back to the huge bed, the cream-and-dark-green duvet reflecting the room's dominant colour scheme.

How many women had shared that bed with Jordan? She recoiled immediately from the insidious question. It was of no concern or interest to her if Jordan chose to spend every night of the week with a different woman. Although somehow she doubted it. One-night stands wouldn't be his style. It was impossible to envisage Jordan living the life of a celibate but he was too fastidious, too selective to be promiscuous. And what exactly was she doing, for heaven's sake, standing in the middle of Jordan's bedroom, speculating on his sex life?

Her gaze fell on a collection of framed photographs displayed on the rosewood writing desk under the sashed window. She hesitated and then berating herself for her weakness gave in to the temptation, drawn irresistibly across the room.

Slowly, she inspected the photographs in turn. Andrew, easily recognizable, his arm around the shoulder of a smiling, curly-headed woman. Jordan's adoptive mother. Tamsin's eyes darkened with compassion for the woman whose life had ended so prematurely in a car crash.

A black Labrador looked up into the camera with soulful brown eyes. Jordan's childhood pet? She didn't even know he liked dogs, had assumed he would regard them merely as an unwanted tie.

Swiftly, she passed over the photograph of an unknown man and woman, her attention caught by a holiday snap of a group of children of mixed ages playing on a beach. She pored over it but if Jordan was amongst them she couldn't identify him. A school trip? Her heart gave an involuntary squeeze. Or an outing from a children's home?

Her forehead furrowed. This collection of photographs indicated a side to Jordan of which she would never have suspected. Yet it was completely characteristic that they weren't displayed in the more public rooms downstairs but here in private, as private as the memories they evidently evoked. Away from inquisitive, prying eyes, she reminded herself guiltily, started to turn away and stiffened.

A youthful, oddly gentle-looking Jordan grinned down at a laughing, dark-haired girl by his side. The colour print must be well over ten years old, but there was no mistaking Jordan's companion. Sara Lyne.

The woman with whom Jordan had once lived. The woman who had evidently remained important enough for him to have kept a constant reminder of her. And now that woman was back in his life....

'I keep my personal correspondence in the drawer on the left. It's not locked.'

Burning with embarrassment and shame, Tamsin spun round and saw Jordan blocking the open doorway, his eyebrows drawn together in a thunderous black line.

'I'm s-sorry,' she muttered inadequately, wondering if she'd ever felt so small in her entire life. 'I opened the door by mistake and...' she faltered, her eyes dilating as he moved purposefully towards her, the ominous expression on his face far from reassuring.

'Jordan, I've said I'm sorry—'

The words strangled in her throat as he reached out an arm and pulled her roughly against him, his mouth covering hers in a brutal, savage kiss that was as punishing as a physical blow. Then raising his head, he spun her around in his arms and ejected her through the open door, slamming it behind her.

Dazed, feeling as if her legs were going to give way, Tamsin stood motionless on the landing. Tentatively, she ran her tongue over her sore, bruised lips. A kiss that had been prompted and executed without desire or passion but purely from anger. And justifiably so....

No! Jordan's action wasn't justifiable or excusable. Did he think he had some open mandate to kiss her, touch her whenever the mood suited him? Adrenalin surging through her, she swung back round, gave a perfunctory knock on the door and burst into the room.

'I'm sick to death of you mauling me about, manhandling me. Okay, I looked at a few lousy photos...that doesn't give you the right to—' She stopped, realizing that she was talking to thin air, and then her eyes flew across the room as she saw Jordan emerging from the *en suite* bathroom. He'd removed his jumper and was in the process of unbuttoning his shirt.

'I'm afraid I missed most of that.' Reaching the final button, he shrugged the shift from his powerful, bronzed shoulders. Bare chested, he turned to face Tamsin. 'I'm just about to take a shower. If you're planning a replay, perhaps you'd care to join me?' Casually, his hand dropped to the buckle of his jeans.

He wouldn't...damn exhibitionist! As she turned and fled down the landing, Tamsin heard the mocking laughter echoing after her. She should have stayed and

THE EDITOR'S "THANK YOU"
FREE GIFTS INCLUDE:

▶ Four BRAND-NEW romance novels
▶ A Cuddly Teddy Bear

DETACH AND MAIL CARD TODAY!

PLACE
FREE GIFT
SEAL
HERE

YES! I have placed my Editor's "thank you" seal in the space provided above. Please send me 4 free books and a Cuddly Teddy Bear. I understand I am under no obligation to purchase any books, as explained on the back and on the opposite page.

116 CIH AZKN (U-H-R-06/96)

NAME

ADDRESS   APT.

CITY   STATE   ZIP

Thank you!

Offer limited to one per household and not valid to current Harlequin Romance® subscribers. All orders subject to approval.

© 1991 HARLEQUIN ENTERPRISES LTD.   PRINTED IN U.S.A.

THE HARLEQUIN READER SERVICE®: HERE'S HOW IT WORKS

Accepting free books places you under no obligation to buy anything. You may keep the books and gift and return the shipping statement marked "cancel". If you do not cancel, about a month later we will send you 6 additional novels, and bill you just $2.67 each plus 25¢ delivery and applicable sales tax, if any*. That's the complete price, and—compared to cover prices of $3.25 each—quite a bargain! You may cancel at any time, but if you choose to continue, every month we'll send you 6 more books, which you may either purchase at the discount price…or return at our expense and cancel your subscription.

*Terms and prices subject to change without notice. Sales tax applicable in N.Y.

If offer card is missing write to: Harlequin Reader Service, 3010 Walden Ave., P.O. Box 1867, Buffalo, NY 14240-1867

BUSINESS REPLY MAIL
FIRST-CLASS MAIL   PERMIT NO. 717   BUFFALO, NY

POSTAGE WILL BE PAID BY ADDRESSEE

HARLEQUIN READER SERVICE
3010 WALDEN AVE
PO BOX 1867
BUFFALO, NY 14240-9952

NO POSTAGE
NECESSARY
IF MAILED
IN THE
UNITED STATES

called his bluff, she thought bitterly, instead of letting him, yet again, reduce her to the level of a stammering, crimson-faced adolescent.

She flung open a door to her right and momentarily forgot everything as she gazed with pleasure at the white sloping ceiling, the delicate pattern of wild flowers on the wallpaper, the warm, glowing oak furnishings. Crossing the thick green carpet, she knelt on the window-seat and gazed out through the latticed window and discovered that the room overlooked the swimming pool, the water shimmering far below in the moonlight.

Unbidden and unwanted, a memory stirred. Jordan patiently teaching her to perform a racing dive, teasing her unmercifully for her ungainly bellyflops into the water. Had the Jordan with the dancing blue eyes, warm, infectious grin ever really existed, she wondered wryly, or simply been a figment of her imagination? She'd spent that whole summer laughing with him... but that too had been an illusion. Jordan hadn't been laughing with her but at her. She winced. Had her ridiculous infatuation been so pathetically obvious?

Kicking off her shoes, she padded across to the *en suite* bathroom, pleasantly surprised to find it was as well-equipped for a guest as a first-class hotel. Thick, fluffy towels were folded neatly over the heated rail and an array of expensive toiletries including toothpaste and sealed brush were displayed on the shelf above the marble basin.

Stripping off her clothes, she had a quick shower and, clad in the white towelling robe she discovered on the back of the door, returned to the bedroom. She frowned, puzzled by the glow of light outside the window, and moved across the carpet to investigate. The floodlights around the pool had been switched on, illuminating the solitary swimmer.

He was mad. Stark, staring mad. Who in their right mind went swimming at this hour of the night or, to be precise, early morning? The water might be heated but it was still only March. Perhaps he was on some sort of macho keep-fit jag....

As Jordan reached the far end and pulled himself out, Tamsin felt her stomach lurch, totally unprepared for her reaction to the almost naked masculine body. For a brief second, he stood poised at the edge of the pool, moonlight playing over the naked width of his shoulders, and then executed a perfect dive back into the water.

Tamsin's breath caught in her throat. Beautiful was normally the last word she would use to describe a man but there was no other adjective to describe the bronzed male form powering himself with effortless ease through the silver water.

Kneeling on the window-seat, chin cupped in her hands, she watched him tumble turn and come back towards her. Her stomach muscles cramped into a fierce, yearning knot. More than anything in the world, she wanted him to look up at her with a slow, lazy grin and invite her to join him in that enchanted moonlit world beyond the window.

And she'd mentally accused Jordan of being deranged! An enchanted world? she mocked herself. Freezing cold water and an equally chilling companion? Abruptly, she pushed herself to her feet, drew the curtains and, removing her robe, padded across to the bed.

Switching off the light, she determinedly closed her eyes, but exhausted as she was, sleep eluded her completely. She stared up into the darkness and then turned over onto her stomach and plumped up the pillow. Restlessly, she curled up on one side and then the other. It was impossible. The oblivion she so desperately craved escaped her completely.

Flicking on the light, she stretched out a hand and selected a book at random from the catholic selection on the bedside table. Resolutely, she opened the covers but the words made no sense, were superimposed with the image of Jordan. Every angle and plane of his face, every fluid line of his body burned in her brain.

Snapping the book closed, she sat up. She just couldn't get comfortable in this damn bed. She was too hot, waves of heat ebbing and flowing through her body. Her breasts ached, felt unnaturally swollen. There was a knot in her lower abdomen twisting tighter and tighter and her stomach kept dipping as if she were at sea in a force ten gale.

Irritably, she tossed back the duvet and padded to the chair where she'd left her clothes. Slipping the baggy T-shirt she'd worn under her jumper over her head, she reached for her jeans and tugged them up over her slim hips. Hot milk. Cocoa. Weren't they the standard remedy for insomnia? Although what she really craved was a long, cold drink to ease the dry tautness in her throat.

She darted over to the window, ascertaining with relief that the outside lights had been turned off, and left the room. The last thing she wanted was to encounter Jordan, for him to think she had deliberately come downstairs in search of him.

Reaching the bottom of the stairs, she headed down the hall towards the kitchen and stopped. The door to her left, which led to the covered passageway connecting to the swimming pool and changing area, was open, light streaming out. So presumably, Jordan was still up after all.

She hesitated. She could just imagine his acerbic comments if he discovered her rummaging around in the kitchen. It might be more diplomatic, not to mention courteous, she admitted grudgingly, to ask him first. Grimacing, she walked through the door, down the passage and through a second door, the carpet underfoot giving way to cream tiles. Directly ahead, French windows gave access out to the darkened swimming pool; to her left, the doors of the four changing rooms, each equipped with a shower, lay open, the interiors deserted.

Process of elimination. Jordan must be in the sauna. Resignedly, she pushed open the fifth door.

'Jordan, may I—' The words froze in her throat as her gaze simultaneously encompassed the brief black swimming trunks discarded in the middle of the tiled floor and the bronzed, naked male body lying stretched out on the wooden slats. Oh, God, why didn't she ever think...?

She couldn't move, remained rooted to the floor, mesmerized by his body, her breath catching in her throat. In the same split second, she recognized her own body's immediate feminine response. Her stomach muscles tightened, her ribcage rose in time to her erratic breathing, lifting her taut breasts, rubbing the swollen nipples against the thin material of her T-shirt.

Then, as Jordan reached for a towel, knotting it around his waist while swinging himself into a sitting position, she broke from her trance.

'I'm sorry...' She didn't need to see the expression on his face to know that her aroused feelings were as tangible as his. But she could do nothing to stop them. Blindly, she turned towards the door.

'Tamsin.'

The urgency in the husky voice halted her. Unsteadily, she turned round, feeling as if her legs would give way as she saw the raw, naked hunger in the dark blue eyes. His gaze dropped, moved to the swell of her breasts, as visible as if the T-shirt was a second skin, his breathing as erratic, as ragged as her own.

'I need to look at you... I need to see you....'

The hoarse words should have shocked her back to reality but they didn't, merely intensified the furnace raging inside her; the knowledge that she could affect Jordan like this was more heady than any drug. Never before had she felt so conscious of her own body and the pleasure it could share with a man. No, she amended dazedly as Jordan moved towards her. Not *a* man. Not *any* man. But this man. Jordan...

She shuddered convulsively as he drew her slowly into his arms, her eyes locking into his, drowning in the blue, shadowy depths. She offered no resistance as he gently eased the T-shirt over her head and dropped it to the floor. Then, at the last minute, the instinct to cover herself in the classic gesture proved too great.

'Put your arms down... look at me.'

Taking a deep breath, Tamsin did as he asked, the open desire in his eyes as they moved over her naked, creamy breasts making the blood roar in her ears.

He reached for the top button of her jeans and then began to draw down the zip, sliding the jeans over her hips. Her breathing grew more and more shallow as she stood motionless in front of him, that wantonness excited to fever pitch as she watched the expression on his face while his eyes caressed her body, lingering over the curve of her taut breasts.

'You're beautiful. So beautiful. Just as I imagined.'

Jordan had imagined her like this.... As he reached out and took hold of her hand, gently drawing her even closer, she felt weak, dizzy with anticipation.

Raising her hand to his mouth, he touched the palm with his lips and then his teeth closed over her index finger, biting it gently before drawing it inside the hot moistness of his mouth. Her eyelashes flickered downwards.

'Jordan...'

He touched her face, traced the outline of her cheekbones, probed the delicate, sensitive whorls of her ear before dropping to her mouth. Her lips parted instinctively, closing over his finger, her tongue moving against it, imitating what he had done to her, his rapid breathing telling her that it gave him equal pleasure.

His hands moved, trailed an expert path down her throat, over the silkiness of her shoulders, dropped to her ribcage and then slowly and languorously circled her breasts, teasing them until they burned from his touch.

'Jordan,' she begged her need, swaying towards him.

'Don't move, Tamsin. Just stand there,' he muttered.

He began a slow, feathery massage over the flat, satin skin of her stomach. Her muscles contracted. She could hardly bear it, this exquisite form of torture. His light, sensuous touch continued and finally moved lower but only to touch her legs, caressing her calves, moving up over her knees and back down again.

'Jordan...' she moaned his name deep in her throat.

'Tamsin.'

It took a second for the husky voice to penetrate her head, her body reeling from shock as the hands that had driven her to fever pitch were now pushing her away. Coherent thought gradually took form, her eyes flickering open. If this had just been another of his power games...if he'd simply set out to humiliate her...

She forced herself to meet his gaze, witnessed the naked passion in the narrowed, half-closed eyes, and despite the warmth from the sauna, she shivered. This was no game.

'I want...I need to make love to you, Tamsin.' His voice was ragged as he rose to his feet, towering above her, seemingly oblivious to the fact that the towel had slipped over his hips to the floor.

This was the time to come to her senses. He was giving her a chance to escape, to back out before it was too late.

Her eyes locked into his, only inches separating her from the satin strength of his body. She could no more walk away now than fly to the moon.

Slowly, she stretched out a hand and touched his face, traced the tenacious line of his jaw, the firm, straight mouth. That longing to feel his mouth against hers, to melt into him, was unendurable.

'Kiss me. Please,' she implored shakily and froze with stunned disbelief as he abruptly pushed her hand away.

'Get out, Tamsin,' he rasped. 'Go.'

She stared at him uncomprehendingly, her eyes wide with shocked confusion. What was happening? Jordan's eyes, his body, flagrantly contradicted those harsh words of dismissal.

'Don't you understand what I've been trying to tell you?' he thundered. 'I hadn't planned...I'm not prepared...and if I start to kiss you, touch you again, I'm not going to be able to stop!'

Comprehension finally dawned, mingled with incredulity that this strong, invincible man should so doubt his own self-control where she was concerned. At the same time came the knowledge that she was glad Jordan wasn't 'prepared', reinforcing her suspicion that his media playboy image was exaggerated, that he wasn't in the habit of indulging in casual sexual encounters.

'Tamsin...for God's sake...go.'

'It's all right.' Her voice cracked, every nerve ending in her body raw, alive to the sexual tension emanating from Jordan. 'I'm on the P-pill,' she mumbled.

As she saw the sudden shadow flit over his face, she stiffened. Was that disapproval? How dare he judge her, condemn her? That the doctor had in fact prescribed the Pill purely to regulate her periods was neither here nor there.

'You damn hypocrite,' she flared. 'You're like something out of the Ark. I didn't think men like you still existed in this day and age....'

Her words choked in her throat as she saw the reflection of her own anger in his eyes. Anger that suddenly erupted into a volcano of desire as their mouths locked together.

Sweeping her up in his arms, Jordan carried her towards the door....

CHAPTER FIVE

As JORDAN set her upright on the carpet by the king-size bed, Tamsin swayed against him, her arms still locked around his neck, her breasts grazing the wall of his chest. Vaguely, she was aware that she was in Jordan's bedroom but had no real recollection of how she'd arrived there. She was no longer capable of rational, coherent thought. There was no past, no future, just this moment in time, this explosion of senses.

She dropped her hands to his shoulders, revelling in the feel of the hard band of muscle beneath her palms, drinking in the scent of his skin as she pressed small, heated kisses over his collar-bone.

'Do you have any idea of what you're doing to me?' Jordan muttered thickly in her ear, his mouth trailing a scalding path down her neck. His hands moved caressingly over her silky skin, sweeping down the length of her back.

'I wanted to take this slowly but I've waited four years and I don't think I can wait much longer.'

'Four years?' Tamsin whispered, her eyes focusing unsteadily on his tense face.

'I wanted you the moment I first saw you.' His lips closed over the pulse at the base of her throat. 'But you were too young, too immature, would have confused desire with love.'

His words took time to register in her befuddled brain . . . too immature to know the difference between desire and love. Something inside her recoiled...but it was too late; she couldn't think straight anymore, was drowning in a whirlpool of alien sensations as his arms tightened around her, moulding her against him.

'Jordan, please.' She heard a voice she hardly recognized as her own pleading desperately. 'Please...' That ache inside her was no longer a teasing build-up of anticipation but a torment that had to be assuaged.

'What do you want, Tamsin?' Jordan muttered hoarsely, raising his head. 'Tell me what you want. Say it out loud.' His eyes blazed into hers like blue fire.

'I w-want you.' She almost sobbed the words out, pride, caution, forgotten in that driving, burning need. 'I want all of you...' She hesitated, stiffening with sudden panic, acutely conscious of her own inexperience, wishing she knew exactly how to please him.

With a muffled groan, Jordan tipped her backwards onto the bed, stretching out beside her. Blindly, Tamsin reached for him, her hands gripping his shoulders, her mouth urgently seeking his. She wanted to share this with him, be part of him....

Slowly, Jordan lowered himself between her thighs. For an infinitesimal second, Tamsin tensed, saw the immediate comprehension in Jordan's eyes as he lay still above her, his breathing ragged.

'Are you all right?' he demanded hoarsely. 'Damn, the last thing I wanted was to hurt you.'

'No...Jordan...p-please don't stop,' she implored as that brief moment of pain changed to shocked pleasure. Nothing had prepared her for this, this frenzied spiral of aching pleasure, their bodies fusing together, moving in unison.

I love you... I love you. The words pounded in her head as she shuddered her release, Jordan's voice hoarse against her breast as he groaned his own heated satisfaction.

Slowly, her muscles started to relax, her breathing returning to normal as she lay in a dreamy cocoon of languid well-being. Gently, her fingers stroked the back of the dark head pressed against her breast, the rush of tenderness flooding through her making her weak.

She loved him. Dazedly, she smiled up at the ceiling. Had always loved him. And whatever happened in the future she would never regret this, wanted to bottle up this moment forever. This feeling of complete and utter peace, of soaring happiness, of absolute rightness, as if this was where she belonged. Jordan's warm breath against her skin, the silkiness of his hair beneath her fingers, the weight of his body against her. If only the world would stop now, if only she could stay like this forever. *I love you... I love you.* She wanted to shout it out at the top of her voice.

As she felt Jordan stir, move away from her onto his side, she slammed her eyes shut. Whatever happened, he must never suspect.

'Tamsin?' Easing himself onto his elbow, Jordan looked down at her, smoothing back the damp tendrils of hair from her forehead.

Her eyes flickered open, the gentle, caressing hand making her skin tingle with soporific pleasure. Reality. Sanity. Post-mortems. She would have the rest of her life for those. She just wanted to cling to this happiness for as long as she could, live in this fool's paradise just a short while longer.

'You haven't slept with Tom,' Jordan murmured slowly, almost disbelievingly.

'I told you we were just friends—'

'Or any other man,' he continued.

Tamsin's mouth curved softly, something inside her melting at the unmistakable gloating satisfaction in his voice. Surely this was more than just masculine ego. He must care something for her. That shadow in his eyes earlier hadn't been disapproval, she suddenly realized, but disappointment. He had wanted her to be a virgin, wanted to be her first man.

'I know.' His straight mouth quirked in an unrepentant grin. 'The original male chauvinist.' He kissed her swiftly on her parted lips before she could agree. 'Your first lover,' he murmured softly and, turning onto his back, pulled her into the crook of his arms, resting his chin on top of her head as it nestled against his chest.

First lover and only lover, Tamsin mused dreamily, smoothing her palms over his chest, fascinated by the texture of his hard, hair-roughened skin. There would never be anyone but Jordan. She suffocated the shooting fear, giving it no time to materialize. Here and now was all that mattered, she reminded herself fiercely. Jordan's arms around her, the beat of his heart in her ear, the feel of his skin beneath her palm, the brush of his long, lean legs against hers. She sighed softly, saturating her senses with him, and then lifted her head.

'Jordan, what happened to your parents?' she asked quietly, instantly regretting the impulsive question as she felt him tense against her, saw a muscle flicker along the line of the strong jaw. She'd spoilt everything. He was going to withdraw from her, block her out. Damn it all. The familiar surge of frustration swept over her. She had just made love with him, was lying naked in his arms. He couldn't just slam down the shutters, retreat behind that brick wall again, treat her as if she were nothing more than a prying busybody.

Pulling herself out of his arms, she eased herself into a sitting position, bracing herself for battle, and was completely disconcerted as she heard the soft chuckle, saw the warm amusement in his eyes.

'Don't take up poker,' he advised. 'Do I irritate you that much?'

'You are the most aggravating person I've ever met in my life!' She looked down into the dark blue eyes, loving him so much it hurt. 'I never know what you're thinking, what you're feeling . . .' Her voice trailing off, she wondered uneasily if she'd given too much away. 'After four years I still don't know anything about you,' she finished lamely.

'Try asking.'

'Every time I do—'

'You fly off the handle without giving me a chance to reply.'

'I do not,' she denied heatedly and caught the mocking grin on his face. She grinned back, desperately trying to ignore that chasm of emptiness opening inside her as she recognized their total incompatibility. Jordan, calm, rational, controlled. And she the complete antithesis. Overemotional, impulsive, ruled by her heart more than her head, given to jumping into a situation with both feet first before ascertaining all the facts. No wonder she grated on him so often.

'My parents,' Jordan murmured quietly, instantly claiming her attention. Folding his arms behind his head, he focused his eyes on the ceiling.

'My mother married my father when she was barely seventeen because she was pregnant with me. She walked out on both of us when I was six. My father was unable to cope and I was taken into the care of the local authority, placed in a foster home and, later, offered up for adoption.'

There wasn't a flicker of emotion either in Jordan's voice or on his face, no trace of self-pity or bitterness. It was as if he was merely relaying an impersonal factual account but it was that very matter-of-factness, the words left unsaid, that made Tamsin's heart squeeze with pain. It was all too unbearably easy to visualize the small, neglected boy, unwanted by both parents, blamed for the forced marriage.

'I was ten when Andrew and Jean adopted me.'

And five years later, his adoptive mother had been killed. Sick with compassion, knowing how inadequate were any words she could offer, Tamsin reacted instinctively, her arms reaching out for him as she slid down beside him. Gently, she stroked back an unruly lock of hair from the high proud forehead, shaken by the surge of fierce protectiveness that swept through her for the boy he had once been.

'I had my parents traced about six years ago,' he suddenly said. 'My father's working in Australia. My mother's remarried with a young family and living in the north.'

'Did you make any attempt to see her?' Tamsin asked quietly.

'I thought about it,' he admitted and then shrugged. 'But in the end I couldn't see what purpose it would serve.'

'Do you hate her?'

He was silent for a second. 'No,' he finally said quietly. 'Not any more.'

'I'm glad.'

For a second he lay inert beside her and then pulled her so tightly against him that she thought she would suffocate. His hold easing, he touched her face, caressing her cheek, the atmosphere between them instantly changing as his eyes locked into hers. She could feel his body hardening against her, her own swift response. Slowly he brushed her lips with his mouth, his fingers sliding through her hair, spreading it like a silky curtain over the pillow.

'Do you know how many times I've imagined you like this? Soft and naked in my bed...' He covered her face in tiny little kisses, his hands moving slowly and languidly down the length of her body as she twisted against him, her arms locking around his neck.

'Not too sore?' he asked gently, eyes dark with concern.

'No,' she assured him, her breathing unsteady.

'This time it will be even better,' he promised, his mouth claiming hers again.

Not better. Different. Curled up beside Jordan, her satiated body flowing with warm lassitude, Tamsin smiled drowsily, watching the dawn flicker into the room. Slow, prolonged, sensuous pleasure. Pleasure given and pleasure received. Learning every inch of Jordan's hard male body with growing assurance and uninhibitedness. Touching, tasting, breathing him. Jordan's mouth, his hands against her skin, bringing her to fever pitch time and time again before that final triumphant ecstasy.

Lifting her head from the pillow, Tamsin looked down at the man lying beside her. Long, dark eyelashes resting on his cheek-bones, his chest moved rhythmically up and down in time to his regular breathing. Unobserved, she let her gaze move over the familiar masculine features, the firm, straight mouth, the strong jawline, angled tenaciously even in sleep. Unable to resist the temptation, she leaned over and kissed his forehead.

'I love you, Jordan Keston,' she whispered softly and settled back into the curve of his arms, her eyes remaining fixed determinedly on his face. She wasn't going to sleep. Wasn't going to waste one second of this precious time. Wanted to hug every second to her, savour it, imprint it in her memory forever. Slowly, her eyelids began to drop downwards.

In the twilight world between sleeping and waking, Tamsin stretched herself luxuriously. She felt wonderful, glowing with blissful contentment. Her eyelashes flickered open and she gazed up at the rays of sunlight dancing on the unfamiliar white ceiling. Her mouth curved gently. Jordan's room...Jordan's bed...

Slowly, she turned her head and discovered the empty pillow beside her. Neither were there any sounds of activity emerging from the open door of the bathroom. Disappointment was tinged with a certain amount of relief as she sat up. She needed some time alone to come to terms with what had happened last night.

Stretching out a hand, she traced the indention in the pillow beside her. The most special, wonderful night of her life. She began to grin inanely as she slipped from the bed. Blinking in surprise and gratitude as she saw her jeans and T-shirt folded neatly over the fireside chair.

She giggled, hoping fervently that it was Jordan responsible for their reappearance and not his housekeeper.

Borrowing Jordan's robe, she gathered up her clothes in her arms and returned to her own room to shower and dress, bursting into laughter as she caught a glimpse of her reflection in the mirror. Was that girl with the idiotic smile, flushed cheeks and glowing eyes really her? She felt different. Complete. Whole. Fired with frenetic energy. She wanted to tell the whole world how she felt and yet at the same time wanted to hug the precious secret to herself.

Humming under her breath, she closed the bedroom door behind her and made her way along the landing and down the stairs. She faltered slightly as she reached the hall, suddenly feeling quite ridiculously nervous as she eyed the dining-room door, visualizing Jordan beyond, eating a leisurely breakfast, surrounded by the Sunday papers. Taking a deep breath, she pushed open the door and froze.

Jordan was standing by the long-lashed window, one hand resting on the shoulder of the dark-haired woman in front of him, the other hand cupped around her chin, lifting her expectant face up towards his.

The bastard. The low-down, stinking bastard! He'd left her in his bed and walked straight into Sara Lyne's arms. It was so incredible she wouldn't have believed it if it hadn't been for the evidence of her own eyes.

'Tamsin.' Jordan greeted her easily as he swung to face her, his hands dropping to his side. 'I thought you were still asleep.'

'Evidently!' He didn't even have the grace to look disconcerted, was actually smiling at her. She wanted to pick up the milk jug and throw it at his head. After emptying the contents over the supercilious, elegant woman by his side. Her legs were shaking so much she thought they would give way and she reached for the support of a chair, her knuckles whitening as her hand gripped the back of it.

'I think I'll take a walk around the garden,' the brunette murmured, touching Jordan's arm lightly with a well-manicured hand, the patronizing amusement in her eyes as she arched a meaningful eyebrow, incensing Tamsin still further. Gliding across the carpet, Sara disappeared through the French window.

Tamsin's eyes darted back to Jordan, her heart thudding painfully as he moved towards her.

'Good morning,' he murmured softly, looking down into her eyes. 'Miss me?' His head lowered towards her.

She jerked her face away, recoiling backwards. 'Don't touch me!' Were she and Sara Lyne completely interchangeable? Didn't he care who he held in his arms as long as they were female? she thought savagely.

He stiffened, his eyes moving slowly over her stony face. 'What's the matter?' he asked quietly, his eyebrows drawing together.

What's the matter? He had the gall to even ask! 'Last night was a mistake.' The biggest mistake of her life. 'And one I have no intention of ever repeating.' Her voice was as brittle as glass.

The passing shadow in his eyes was so fleeting she decided she must have imagined it.

'I see.' Swinging away from her, he strode over to the window.

Tamsin stared rigidly at his back. He didn't care a damn. Last night had meant nothing more to him than a few hours of transitory physical pleasure and it was a matter of complete indifference to him whether they were repeated. As he had already illustrated, she was easily replaceable.

'Couldn't you at least have waited until I was out of the house?' she exploded. The chair crashed against the table dislodging a bowl, which tumbled to the floor and disintegrated. 'Were you even going to change the damn sheets?'

He turned round, a muscle flickering along the line of his jaw. 'You think Sara and I—'

'I don't *think* ... I'm not blind....' She gulped for breath.

'I'm flattered by your assumption that I'm some sort of sexual athlete,' he drawled, but the casualness in his tone was belied by the dangerous glint in his eyes. Sauntering across the room, he dropped to his haunches and picked up the fragments of broken china and placed them on the table. 'Pity. I rather liked it.' Abruptly, he spun round to face her. 'What were you expecting this morning?' he rasped. 'A declaration of undying love and devotion?'

'Don't be so damn ridiculous! Of course not.' Her eyes sparked back into his. 'But I did expect some sort of consideration ... didn't expect you to go flaunting your—'

'My what, Tamsin?' he intervened, his voice low and ominous. 'And if anyone did the flaunting—'

'What?' she screeched.

'You turn up at my home uninvited in the middle of the night, prowl around in the early hours looking for me—'

'I wasn't looking for you! I was thirsty—'

'And naturally the obvious place to look for a drink was the sauna?' he taunted derisively. 'You did all the running, Tamsin, made it blatantly clear what you wanted.' He shrugged. 'And I'm only human. We had sex. Spent a few enjoyable hours together. End of story.'

Had sex. Not made love. Silently, Tamsin screamed her protest. How could he reduce everything to such a basic, sordid level, sully forever the memory of last night. The pain in her chest was so intense it was as if he'd stabbed her with a knife. He'd exhibited not just passion last night, but warmth, tenderness, an unselfish constraint—and it had all been part of the expert act. A sham. Her throat was scalding from the unshed tears. If only he hadn't made her feel so special....

His face was like a mask, his eyes cool, dismissive. He felt absolutely nothing for her, not even liking or respect. She'd just been a compliant body.

'You used me.' She felt sick.

He threw back his head and laughed. 'Oh, come on, Tamsin, not that old chestnut. I didn't persuade you into my bed with a lot of fairy tales. You went willingly. In fact, as I recall it, rather more than willingly. Eagerly.' He paused, his eyes raking her face. 'Take a tip, Tamsin. Women's lib or not, men still like to do the chasing.'

'And that's all sex is to you, isn't it? A challenge. A game.' She raised her eyes to his. 'I feel sorry for you, Jordan. Oh, you're rich, successful, good-looking, but that's only superficial trappings. Inside you're cold and empty. Nothing.'

'The feeling of disillusionment is mutual, Tamsin,' he returned evenly. 'I think you have the loveliest eyes I've ever seen in my life. And the tragedy is that all that lies behind them is a petty, shallow little mind.' He moved to the door and paused. 'Sara Lyne dropped in this morning because she had some papers for me to sign, that's all. Contrary to what your sordid little imagination had conjured up, we were not indulging in some post-cornflakes foreplay when you barged in. I was merely removing an eyelash from one of Sara's eyes.'

Oh, God. Tamsin felt the colour burn her cheeks. How could she have been such a fool?

'That makes two of us,' Jordan said quietly and she jolted as once again he'd exhibited the uncanny ability to read her thoughts. 'I actually thought after last night we could finally stop fighting. Make a fresh start, spend a lazy, peaceful day together.'

She looked at him uncertainly. This was just some new tactic, some new trap.

With a sudden gesture of weary defeat, Jordan held up his hands in front of him. 'But peace is the last thing you'd ever be capable of giving a man, isn't it, Tamsin?' Silently, he opened the door and disappeared into the hall.

CHAPTER SIX

MECHANICALLY Tamsin pulled out the chair and sank into it, staring unseeingly down at the white tablecloth. She'd ruined everything. How could she have demeaned herself by ranting and raving at him as she had, the archetypal jealous, possessive woman? Even throwing in the standard line about being used... So much for pride, dignity, composure. And her suspicions and accusations had all been unfounded.

Oh, come on, you didn't really fall for the last little spiel, she taunted herself. Genuinely believe that Jordan's relationship with Sara Lyne was purely platonic, that he'd seriously planned to spend the day with her? It was just another of his little wind-ups. Engineered to make her feel that she was in the wrong. Peace! she scoffed. The last thing she could imagine Jordan wanting in his life was peace. He spent his life in the fast lane, thrived on the ruthless cut and thrust of the business world. Peace? He'd be bored to death.

Her eyes darkened. Jordan had spent the formative years of his life in the battle zone between two warring parents. Memories of Jordan sitting in the kitchen with her mother, the expression of complete tranquillity on his face, unfurled in her head. It was her mother's serenity that had always attracted him, she realized with a jolt. A serenity, an inner calmness that her volatile daughter didn't possess.

She lifted her head and stiffened, watching Sara Lyne stroll across the immaculate lawn beyond the French windows. A few seconds later, she was joined by Jordan. Tamsin swallowed. She couldn't hear what they were saying but didn't need to. The expressions on their faces, their complete absorption in each other said it all. Oh, sure, Jordan, Sara just came over to get some papers signed, just happened to have something in her eye!

As they disappeared from view behind a large oak tree, her jaw clenched so hard together her teeth ached. Well, the brunette had a far more forgiving nature than she had, because she wouldn't touch Jordan Keston with a bargepole now. It wasn't until she tasted salt on her lips that she realized that she was crying.

'Morning, Tamsin love. His lordship said you were down.'

Swiftly dabbing at her face, she twisted her head round and smiled brightly at Jordan's middle-aged housekeeper.

'Good morning, Mrs. Duncan. I like the new hair-style.' She was amazed at the control in her voice.

'Thought I'd go blonde and bubbly for summer,' the older woman returned comfortably, patting the bleached curls. 'Jim's not so keen,' she added as an afterthought, referring to her good-natured, long-suffering husband, who acted as gardener, general handyman and occasional chauffeur. 'Prefers me as a passionate redhead or sultry brunette.' She threw back her head and roared with self-mocking laughter.

Tamsin found it impossible not to grin back. She'd always liked the forthright, flamboyant woman although she'd often considered her unswerving devotion to Jordan to be misplaced.

'Now what would you like for breakfast?'

'Just coffee, please.' Food would choke her the way she felt right now.

'Poached egg and toast,' Mrs. Duncan contradicted her benevolently. She beamed. 'Grapefruit or cereal to start with?'

'Grapefruit, please.' Tamsin beamed back, admitting defeat, and then as the housekeeper spotted the broken bowl, confessed, 'That was me, I'm afraid.'

'Been fighting again? Chuck it at his head?'

'Not quite. Though I was tempted,' Tamsin admitted brightly as the housekeeper disappeared through the door.

Been fighting again. Miserably, Tamsin stared out into the garden. That about summed up her relationship with Jordan. Perpetual, unceasing conflict. Her heart gave a dull thud. Physical intimacy hadn't brought them closer; perversely it seemed to have widened that unbridgeable gap between them.

'There you are, love.'

She forced her features into a smile as Mrs. Duncan returned from the kitchen and placed the fresh segmented grapefruit and a tray of coffee in front of her.

'Thank you.' She gazed down at the plate, her stomach instantly rebelling, her throat constricting at the thought of trying to swallow anything. Her small chin squared stubbornly. Damn it! She was not going to go into a decline, wilt and wail over a mere male. And certainly not over Jordan Keston. Determinedly, she picked up her spoon, her resolution wavering as Jordan and Sara came into view again, the latter's hand tucked possessively through Jordan's arm.

'Certainly staking her claim, isn't she?' Mrs. Duncan observed drily, following Tamsin's gaze. 'She came waltzing in this morning as if she owned the place, demanding I go upstairs and wake Jordan up.'

Tamsin averted her face quickly but it was too late. The other woman had seen the betraying tell-tale flush in her cheeks.

'Oh, heavens . . . you were in bed with him. . . .'

'Mrs. Duncan—'

'I did wonder when Jordan told me you'd stopped over. But I hoped I was wrong and that you'd only stayed because you didn't fancy spending the night in an empty house with your mother away—'

'Mrs. Duncan . . .' Tamsin protested again but the warm, genuine concern on the plump face proved her undoing. She swallowed hard, fighting the temptation to fling herself into the motherly arms like a three-year-old and bawl her eyes out.

'Look, I know it's none of my business, love, but just be careful. Don't go falling in love with him.' She paused. 'He's not the settling-down kind and you are,' she said gently. 'He can't even settle in one place for more than two minutes. Jim and I have been with him for nearly thirteen years and I can't tell you the number of times we've moved house. Up and down England, Paris, Geneva, New York. Keeping Swallow Lodge for four years has been an all-time record.'

Houses, never homes, Tamsin reflected slowly. Bases in which to eat and sleep, entertain. Jordan was too self-sufficient, too restless to need or want any form of permanency in his life be it a place or a person.

'Don't you mind continually being uprooted?' she asked the housekeeper curiously.

'Oh, no, Jim and I love it. Seeing a bit of the world. Never a chance to get bored.' Her eyes softened. 'And I've worked for worse.'

Really? Tamsin mused caustically to herself and frowned. Perhaps Jordan simply had a low boredom threshold, needed the constant stimulation and challenge of new places, new people. Except maybe once...

Jordan and Sara were approaching the house. She glanced at Mrs. Duncan, whose attention like her own was focused outside, and hesitated. She oughtn't to gossip about Jordan with his housekeeper...oh, damn it, why not? She didn't owe him anything.

'Jordan told me they used to live together,' she said with studied casualness.

'Is that a fact?' Mrs. Duncan's eyebrows shot up in surprise. 'Well, it must have been before my time.' She paused as if unwilling to continue and then sighed. 'She's always been around somewhere in the background ever since Jim and I came to work for him. I think she's the only woman who's ever really mattered to him,' she added reluctantly. 'I can't understand why but—' She broke off swiftly as the French windows opened and the subject of their discussion entered the room.

Equally swiftly, Tamsin dropped her eyes to her plate and then surreptitiously studied Jordan from under her thick lashes. He didn't even glance at her.

'Mrs. Duncan, I'm sorry but I won't be in for lunch today after all,' he said courteously and smiled down at the woman by his side. 'I'll just make those phone calls, Sara, and then I'll be with you. Coffee?'

'Yes, please.'

He moved to the door and paused to address his housekeeper again. 'Would you ask Jim to give Tamsin a lift to the station as soon as she's finished breakfast, please?'

What? Tamsin almost tipped the grapefruit into her lap. He was talking about her as if she were nothing more than a piece of unwanted luggage to be disposed of as quickly as possible.

For the first time, Jordan looked at her directly, his eyes like ice. Then pulling out a wad of notes from the pocket of his jeans, he tossed them onto the table. 'You'll need that for the train fare.' Turning on his heel, he strode from the room.

In the abrupt silence that followed his departure, Tamsin was acutely aware that she was the focus of two pairs of eyes, one outraged on her behalf, the other smug, condescending, both waiting expectantly for her reaction.

Her face completely impassive, she picked up her spoon and resumed eating her grapefruit. Sorry. Floor show's cancelled. She could almost feel the disappointment in the air.

'Bring my coffee through to the drawing room, please.' Sara Lyne moved to the door. 'And the Sunday papers,' she added over her shoulder.

'At once, your ladyship!' Mrs. Duncan muttered under her breath, touching her forelock as the door closed. She turned to Tamsin, her eyes both puzzled and sympathetic. She seemed to be about to say something and then, much to Tamsin's relief, changed her mind and picked up the empty dish of grapefruit.

'I think I'll skip the egg and toast.' Tamsin tried to grin but her lips wouldn't move properly.

Mrs. Duncan nodded without protest and walked silently from the room.

Mechanically, Tamsin poured out a cup of coffee, and then stared down into the steaming brown liquid. She wished she could feel angry because that might anesthetize the tearing pain inside her. But she just felt totally drained and empty.

She knew last night had meant nothing to Jordan, that *she* meant nothing to him. But there had been no need to press that point home with such calculated cruelty, she thought dully, make it publicly and humiliatingly clear that her continuing presence in his house was unwanted. She took a long sip of coffee, felt the warmth radiating through her.

She jerked her head up. How dare he treat her like this? His behaviour was unpardonable and she had done absolutely nothing to warrant it. She had made no demands on him, expected nothing from him this morning but common courtesy, civility. And instead, he had treated her as if... Her eyes fell on the wad of notes still lying on the table and nausea gripped her throat.

'Tam?'

She hadn't heard the door open behind her, and for a second, thought she'd imagined the familiar, hesitant voice. Pushing back her chair, she jumped to her feet and spun round.

'Tom! What on earth are you doing here?' Their awkward parting seemed to belong to another lifetime. All she could think of was just how glad she was to see his familiar, dependable face. 'What are you doing here?' she repeated.

The welcome on her face seemed to reassure him and he grinned ruefully. 'I woke up this morning with the vague memory of a bad dream.' He grimaced. 'Only when I saw your note in the kitchen, I realized that it wasn't a dream. I tried to phone you at your mother's house but there was no answer, and then I found your house keys and purse on the hall table.' He paused. 'I guessed you might be here. I tried getting hold of Jordan's number but he's ex-directory—' he grinned '—and the operator seemed oddly resistant to my boyish charm.'

Tamsin grinned back.

'So I decided to shoot on over on the off chance you were here.' Digging into the pocket of his navy windcheater, he placed the keys and purse on the table. 'Thought you'd probably be needing them.'

'Thanks,' she said quietly. In the stark light of day, she couldn't understand what had possessed her to flee the flat the night before, wished with all her heart she hadn't.

'Have you and Jordan been fighting again? He looked like thunder just now when he opened the door to me. I thought he was going to slam it in my face and then he just growled something under his breath and more or less shoved me in the direction of this room.'

'His usual hospitable, courteous self,' Tamsin muttered acidly. *Have you and Jordan been fighting again?* Mrs. Duncan, now Tom . . . She was suddenly conscious of the silence, the tension on his face.

'About last night . . .'

'Forget it.'

'I'd rather clear the air,' he said quietly and, pacing over to the window, looked out into the garden for a moment before turning back to face her. 'I've always liked you, Tamsin. You know that and I can't deny that for a while I hoped that we might become more than just friends. But you never encouraged me or led me to

believe that you wanted anything more than friendship.'
He paused. 'And I suppose deep down I always knew
it was Jordan....'

Tamsin's eyes widened. 'That isn't true!' How could
he possibly have known? She hadn't admitted it to herself
until last night.

'You're the warmest, most fair-minded, tolerant
person I've ever met in my life,' Tom continued quietly.
'You accept people for what they are, warts and all. I've
never heard you criticize anyone.' He paused. 'With one
notable exception. Jordan Keston. I always knew when
you'd seen him because you used to come tearing into
the flat in a steaming temper, running him down. It was
as if you'd undergone some personality change....'

'Personality clash, more like it,' Tamsin muttered
under her breath.

'I'd never known anyone affect you like that before.
I mean, the poor guy couldn't do anything right.'

'Jordan Keston? Poor guy? You don't want to waste
any sympathy on a cold-blooded, unfeeling—'

'And you love him,' he said quietly.

'No!' she denied and looked into the honest dark
brown eyes. 'Yes...I don't know,' she whispered. How
could she love him when she didn't even like him?
Loathed him in fact. Had she fallen into the trap Jordan
had warned her against, simply confused physical attraction, desire, with love? 'I just don't know,' she repeated huskily.

'Did you sleep with him last night?'

She was startled by the blunt question, one she would
never have expected from Tom. Then she felt resentful.
Why did everyone seem to think they had *carte blanche*
to discuss her sex life? Why didn't she just put an ad in

the personal column and have done with it? Then she saw the pain in his eyes.

'Oh, Tom...' Without warning, the tears started to cascade down her cheeks, and the next second, with no real recollection of how it had happened, she was in his arms, her head pressed into his shoulder, sobbing for the pain she had caused him, sobbing for her own pain.

'Here,' Tom murmured softly, pushing a handkerchief into her hands.

'Thanks.' She dabbed at her cheeks. 'You're the best friend I've ever had,' she mumbled, belatedly remembering that she shouldn't be in his arms. She lifted her head and in that moment saw the silent figure standing in the doorway. For a second, blue eyes locked into hazel ones and then he was gone. How long had Jordan been standing there...? She eased herself from Tom's arms. 'Sorry,' she said awkwardly.

'What are friends for?' he returned lightly and then abruptly turned away from her.

'Tom?' she said tentatively.

'It's no good, Tamsin,' he muttered. 'I came over this morning, convinced that I could just carry on being friends with you, but I can't.' He turned round to face her and the expression on his face made her heart squeeze. 'I love you,' he said simply.

Tamsin looked back at him with large, unhappy eyes, wishing with every fibre of her being that she could tell him that his feelings were reciprocated.

'I suppose I've kidded myself for a long time that one day you'll feel the same, but I'm wasting my time, aren't I?'

'Yes.' Tamsin managed to force the word out, knowing that at the very least she owed him the truth.

He nodded and moved across to the door. 'I'm going to take a week's leave and stay with my parents in Cornwall.'

And by the time he returned she would have left the flat, started her new job. 'Tom,' she said unsteadily, 'I do care about you and always will.'

'I know, Tam,' he said wryly. 'As a friend. But it's just not enough for me anymore.'

Silently, she picked up her keys and purse and followed him out of the house and across the gravel sweep to his car.

'Good luck, Tam.' He opened the driver's door and paused before getting in. 'Be happy.' He hesitated, then reaching out a hand, he gently touched her cheek and dived into the car.

Aching with misery, Tamsin watched him disappear down the drive, still not really able to believe that he was departing from her life for good. Had she just made the second biggest mistake of her life? she suddenly wondered desperately. Had her infatuation for Jordan blinded her to her real feelings for Tom? Because that was all she felt for Jordan, she told herself harshly. A ridiculous, pathetic infatuation.

'A reconciliation with the faithful swain?'

She spun round and saw Jordan a few feet behind her, the mockery in his eyes fuelling the anger that had been instantly ignited by the derision in his voice.

'Tom is the kindest, most considerate man I have ever met.' Her voice shook with the effort of controlling the decibels. 'He's worth a million of you.' Spinning on her heel, she marched down the drive and turned into the lane.

It wasn't until she was almost home that she remembered that she had omitted to say goodbye to Mrs. Duncan. Neither, she reminded herself with a rising well of hysteria, had she thanked her host for his hospitality.

'The removal men arrived on time this morning and everything went like clockwork,' Tamsin assured her mother the following evening, doodling absently on the note pad by the telephone.

She'd packed her mother's remaining clothes and personal possessions the previous afternoon and taken them down to Swallow Lodge. Relieved to discover Jim Duncan working in the garden, which had saved her the necessity of going up to the house and possibly encountering Jordan, she'd handed the suitcases over to him and beaten a hasty retreat.

'How's Andrew?'

'Much better. If all goes well, he should be discharged by the end of the week and be able to fly home to recuperate.'

'I'm so pleased.' Tamsin smiled down at the receiver and then stuck out her tongue at the two dark-haired boys who tapped her gently on the head with their squash rackets as they passed her *en route* to the front door.

'Coming down to the club later for a drink?' the taller of the two mouthed at her.

Tamsin shook her head. 'Going to have an early night,' she mouthed back.

'We've decided to postpone the wedding for a few weeks, though,' her mother continued in her ear. 'So I'm flying back on Wednesday to start sorting everything out.'

'Would you like me to meet you at the airport?'

'Thanks, darling, but actually, Jordan organized everything while he was over here.'

Tamsin's fingers tightened around the pencil in her hand. 'Jordan's been out to Geneva?' she said lightly.

'He came over today for a few hours.'

'I suppose he had some business to attend to and combined it with a visit to the hospital,' Tamsin muttered acidly before she could stop herself.

'Jordan came out to see his father,' her mother said quietly, the gentle reproof in her voice unmistakable. 'He's also been very kind to me.' She paused. 'I'll see you soon, darling.'

'Give my love to Andrew. Bye, Mum. Take care.'

Slowly, Tamsin replaced the receiver back on the hook and jolted as she looked down and saw Jordan's name scrawled repeatedly across the note pad. How adolescent could she get! Jerkily, she ripped the page from the book and tore it up into tiny pieces, depositing them in the bin in the kitchen on her way back to the sitting room.

Curling up on the sofa, slim, jean-clad legs tucked under her, she picked up the sandwich she'd been eating before her mother's phone call, and gazed wistfully around the familiar room. She was going to miss this flat, miss the constant, good-natured bantering of her flatmates, and most of all she was going to miss Tom.

Tom... Her eyes darkened unhappily. He was everything that Jordan wasn't. Loyal. Thoughtful. Understanding. She should have given their relationship a proper chance...perhaps even now it wasn't too late....

Springing to her feet, she prowled around the room and paused by the window, staring out into the narrow, car-lined street. She ought to be excited, looking forward to the challenge of a new job, a new home, new experiences and people, but instead she felt uncertain, unsettled, strangely rootless. She liked some degree of permanency in her life, she realized slowly, didn't much like change. Unlike Jordan. Words like stability, security, would be anathema to him....

She spun away from the window. Why did everything always have to come back to Jordan? Why couldn't she just tear him out of her head? Concentrate on Tom. Aware of the growing darkness outside, she flicked on a table lamp and flung herself down on the sofa. Determinedly, she picked up the novel she was currently reading but found it impossible to concentrate. Tossing it aside, she folded her hands behind her head and stared up at the ceiling and groaned as she heard the doorbell. Company was the last thing she felt like at the moment.

Unenthusiastically, she padded over to the window and peeped around the curtain to the pavement below and tensed in disbelief as she saw the familiar tall figure. It was as if thinking about him had somehow conjured up the reality.

As Jordan glanced up, she darted back, chewing her lip, her eyes cloudy with indecision. The doorbell rang again more insistently.

Padding out into the hall, she pressed the intercom. 'Yes?' she enquired coolly.

'May I come in?'

She swallowed. Just the sound of his voice and her pulse rate seemed to have accelerated, she thought with self-disgust. 'Who is it?' she asked frigidly.

'Don't be childish, Tamsin.'

Her lips compressed together. 'Actually, I was just about to—'

'Wash your hair?' he enquired sardonically. He paused. 'We need to talk,' he said quietly.

She hesitated for a second and released the outer door. Then despising herself but unable to resist, she sped into the bathroom and surveyed herself in the mirror with a grimace. No make-up. Hair pulled back in a pony-tail. Over-large striped rugby shirt. Faded denim jeans. *Vogue* magazine, eat your heart out.

As the chimes of the doorbell heralded Jordan's arrival, she took a calming breath and made her way down the flight of stairs to the front door of the flat.

Flinging open the door, she surveyed the towering, dark-suited figure coolly. 'So what did you want to talk to me about?' She made no move to invite him in. He could say what he'd come to say and go, as far as she was concerned.

She saw a muscle clench along the line of his jaw, his eyes as dark as the navy blue tie nestling against the brilliant white shirt.

'You never give an inch, do you, Tamsin? I don't know why the hell I bothered to come!'

'So why did you?' she enquired frigidly.

'To apologize, damn it!'

'Apologize?' she echoed in disbelief. Whatever she'd expected, it wasn't this.

'For my behaviour towards you on Sunday morning,' he thundered. 'And I'm damned if I'm discussing this on the doorstep.' Moving past her into the hall, he slammed the front door behind him and started striding up the stairs.

Tamsin shot after him two steps at a time. 'And this is how you normally apologize?' She charged into the sitting room behind him. 'Barging uninvited into people's homes? Shouting?'

He had taken up a position with his back to the fireplace, arms folded across his deep chest, his stance assuredly and arrogantly male. And that was his idea of looking contrite?

He stared at her stony face, and suddenly his lips twitched. 'I haven't had a lot of practice,' he conceded.

'Well, your technique certainly needs working on!' She ignored the sudden dipping of her stomach, refused to be disarmed by his rueful grin.

'I'm sorry for the way I treated you on Sunday.' He raised a quizzical eyebrow.

'An improvement, I suppose,' she muttered grudgingly. Slowly, she searched his face. 'Why?' she asked abruptly.

'Why did I act the way I did?' He raised his hands and dropped them in a gesture of defeat. 'It's just that you make me so mad sometimes,' he said wryly. 'You came storming into the dining room on Sunday, virtually accusing me of leaping out of your bed into Sara's.'

Tamsin felt the colour tinge her cheeks.

'It was damn insulting to all three of us,' he said quietly and then suddenly gave a snort of laughter. 'You didn't seriously think I was engaged in some sort of sexual marathon, did you? Seeing how many notches I could score on my bedpost in twenty-four hours?'

The colour deepened in Tamsin's face. 'Right, if you've quite finished,' she snapped.

'No, I haven't. And for heaven's sake, sit down and stop hovering over me like a miniature bouncer.'

'Don't tell me to sit down in my own home!' she flared and promptly sank down into the nearest armchair.

Slowly and deliberately, Jordan pulled the companion chair around to face her and folded his long frame into its well-worn depths. The lamp was behind his head, casting a shadow over the chiselled features. He looked tired, she observed, noticing for the first time the lines of strain etched around his eyes and mouth. He must have come straight from the airport.

She dropped her gaze, her heart constricting painfully, the longing to reach out a hand and soothe those lines of tension from his face almost unbearable. She was so sick of always having to fight, to battle, to pretend.... Get a grip on yourself, she ordered herself brusquely. Don't drop your defences.

'We have to talk,' he said quietly and, as she opened her mouth, held up a restraining hand. 'No more point scoring,' he said wearily. 'Talk.' He paused. 'Saturday night changed everything between us.'

Tamsin went rigid, her gaze instantly dropping to the patterned carpet. 'Saturday night was a mistake,' she said evenly. 'One of those things,' she said, shrugging casually.

She was acutely conscious of the silence in the room, of Jordan's eyes on her face, compelling her to look at him. Slowly, she lifted her head, her eyes drawn to his like a magnet. She felt like a rabbit caught in the glare of headlights, mesmerized, immobilized, drowning in those dark, shadowy blue depths.

'Is that all it was, Tamsin?' he said softly. 'One of those things?'

'No!' Tearing her eyes away from his, she leaped to her feet and glared at him. 'It was wonderful! The most wonderful thing that has ever happened to me. All right?' she yelled. 'Is that what you wanted to hear? How damn terrific you are? Satisfied now?' Whirling away, she moved over to the window and stared blindly out into the gathering darkness.

'Tamsin?'

She didn't hear him cross the carpet, froze as she felt him touch her shoulder.

'Look, you've had your evening's entertainment. Just go, will you?' she muttered.

'Stop being so damn touchy. Prickles? A hedgehog is a soft, cuddly toy compared to you!' His hand tightening on her shoulder, he swung her round to face him. 'Is that why you think I'm here? To have my fragile male ego massaged?'

'I don't know why you're here,' she flung back. 'I never know what motivates you, what goes on in your head!' She came to an abrupt halt, her eyes dilating as she saw the expression in his eyes, saw them drop to her mouth. He was so close she could feel the warmth of his breath on her face, her own chest rising and falling in time to his unsteady, ragged breathing.

'You're like a damn rash that won't go away,' he muttered hoarsely, 'itching away under my skin.'

She could hear her heart hammering beneath her ribcage, the blood pounding in her ears, the expression in his eyes making her light-headed. She licked her lips. 'What are you trying to say?'

'What the hell do you think I'm trying to say? That since Saturday night I haven't been able to think about anything else but this....' With a muffled groan, his mouth took possession of hers. 'Now do you understand?' he muttered throatily, looking down into her dazed eyes.

She couldn't think straight. Couldn't believe that this was happening. The blood raced to her head, making her dizzy, weak. Then the adrenalin tore through her in frenetic bursts of tingling elation, her mouth curving in an idiotic smile as she gazed up at him. 'But all we ever do is fight....'

'Except in bed,' he said softly, his eyes dark, opaque pools. His hands slipped to her waist, pulling her towards him. 'Oh, God, I want you....'

It was as if she'd been woken from a trance, shocked back to harsh reality with cold, douching water. How could she have been such a damn little fool to have misconstrued even for a second what Jordan had been saying, misread that expression in his eyes? Her reflexes took over instinctively, her eyelashes dropping over her eyes, the muscles in her face forcing her features into impassivity.

'You want to go to bed with me again?' she said coolly. Deliberately, she turned the knife even deeper in the open, raw wound. 'To have sex?'

She felt him stiffen against her, his eyebrows knitting in a dark line across his forehead. 'To be lovers.'

She felt a surge of hysteria welling inside her. Lovers! Of all the inapposite, ludicrous words. Caring, liking, let alone love, had nothing to do with what he was proposing. Just the cold-blooded satiation of physical desire. Even as her mind recoiled, she could feel her body responding to him, urging her to capitulate, to forget everything but...

No! She jerked her eyes open, tilted her head upwards. 'And how long would this...um...relationship last?'

'I wasn't suggesting we exchange contracts.' A muscle flickered along the line of the hard jaw. 'I'm not asking for a lifetime commitment, Tamsin.'

Just a casual affair based solely on sexual attraction. Her eyelids dropped protectively over her eyes. 'Isn't this going to get a little complicated when I'm working for you?' How could you do this to me, Jordan? she screamed silently with pain. 'Sleeping with the boss?'

She felt his arms slacken their hold. 'I thought you understood,' he said quietly. 'Obviously you won't be able to take up your position with Lyne Air.'

'No, of course not. Obviously.' No job. And in a week, a month...no Jordan. She'd be left with nothing. She pulled herself free from his arms and took a step backwards. 'So I have a choice?' She looked at him squarely and then fished out an imaginary coin from her pocket, tossing it in the air. 'Heads I sleep with you, tails I work for you.' She paused. 'Tails, Jordan,' she said evenly.

'Right. I'll expect you at the airport next Monday at nine o'clock.' He moved toward the door. 'One of the girls in Ops is looking for a new flatmate. Shall I ask her to get in touch with you?'

'Yes, please.' She looked at him in disbelief. His face was a bland mask, his voice brisk and impersonal, devoid of all emotion. A few seconds ago, he'd asked her to be his lover...how could anyone switch on and off so quickly?

He disappeared into the hall and a few seconds later Tamsin heard the sound of the front door slamming.

Slowly, she forced her trembling legs over to the sofa and sank down into the cushions, anger and hurt warring for supremacy. And somewhere mixed in the confusion was the perverse, irrational feeling of deflation that Jordan had given in so easily, hadn't even attempted to dissuade her from her decision.

CHAPTER SEVEN

'THAT'S two seats confirmed on the 1830 flight to Leeds this evening, Mr. Roberts. Your tickets will be waiting for you on departure at the check-in desk.' Replacing the telephone receiver, Tamsin quickly completed the entry on her computer screen and then turned her attention back to the batch of ticket coupons in front of her, sorting them out into numerical order.

Frowning with concentration, she entered the relevant details from each coupon onto a large sheet of ruled paper and then, reaching for a calculator, swiftly added up each column of figures, checking to ensure that their totals balanced.

She glanced up as the door of the reservations office opened, and smiled in greeting at the dark-haired airhostess.

'May I have a travel form? I've just swopped rosters and I've two days off so I thought I'd try and get over to Guernsey.' She perched on the end of the desk. 'All on your own?'

'Mary and Simone are organizing things in the new office.'

'Getting ready for the big day?'

Tamsin nodded with a grin. In four days' time, Lyne Air would commence operating scheduled services under its out-route licence and handling its own passengers, a service currently undertaken by the airport authority. In addition, the reservations department was being transferred from the administration block to new larger offices in the terminal, where it would be more accessible to the public and incorporate a general enquiries desk.

'When do you want to travel?' Tamsin returned to her chair and swivelled to face the VDU. 'I'll check the loads.'

'Going out this afternoon if possible. If I dash home and throw some things in a bag, I should just make the three-thirty. Coming back Wednesday.' Looking out of the window, the hostess suddenly heaved a theatrical sigh. 'What I would give to trade places with her!'

Instinctively, Tamsin glanced up and saw Jordan approaching the building, Sara Lyne by his side.

'They arrived in the same car yesterday morning.' The other girl grinned knowingly.

Tamsin dropped her gaze swiftly back to the computer screen, determinedly ignoring both the cramping of her stomach muscles and the innuendo. Just because Jordan and Sara had arrived at work together, it didn't automatically mean... He may have simply picked her up *en route* to the airport.

'And my flatmate saw them having dinner together last Friday at the Old Beams.'

'Wednesday's wide open inbound,' Tamsin muttered, her hands skimming unsteadily over the keyboard. Sara and Jordan were business partners. It was inevitable that they should spend a great deal of time together. Her heart constricted. Including candlelit dinners in romantic eighteenth-century inns? 'But I think this afternoon's full.' She pressed her lips together, squaring her chin unconsciously. Sara Lyne and Jordan Keston were welcome to each other. She didn't care a hoot. 'No,' she corrected, forcing her attention back to the screen. 'There's been a last-minute cancellation so there's one seat left at the moment. You might be lucky.'

The air-hostess smiled. 'Could you block off the seat?'

Tamsin hesitated, baulking immediately at the other girl's request. Booking the seat in a fictitious name ensured that there would be a free seat on the flight, even though the airline might lose the revenue of a full-paying passenger as a consequence.

'I'm sorry, but I can't do that,' she said quietly and saw the other girl frown.

'Simone always does it,' she insisted, referring to the reservations supervisor.

Tamsin didn't answer.

'Oh, well, I'll just ask her when she gets back.' The hostess picked up her form and flounced out of the office.

Tamsin sighed. Perhaps blocking off seats for staff was a common practice at Lyne Air to which the hierarchy turned a blind eye but somehow she doubted it. She picked up the internal phone as it buzzed in front of her.

'Res office.'

'May I speak to Simone, please?'

Her hand tightened convulsively around the receiver as she recognized the assured, authoritative voice.

'She's over in the new office.'

'Right. Thanks.'

The line went dead. Slowly, Tamsin replaced the receiver. Jordan's voice had been as impersonal as if she'd been a stranger. No, she amended wryly. An employee. Which is exactly how he had treated her over the past three weeks.

Their contact had been minimal, but on the occasions that he had appeared in either the operations or reservations offices between which she'd been dividing the bulk of her time, never once had the expression on his face or the tone of his voice indicated that she was anything more than another member of the Lyne Air staff.

She rose to her feet. Her rejection of his proposition hadn't even dented his male pride, let alone anything else. He had simply dismissed her completely from his thoughts and his life. But then, what else had she expected him to do? She had held a transitory physical attraction for him, that's all.

Moving over to the large table by the window, she surveyed the boxes of summer timetables and fares without enthusiasm. She'd been working on the mail shot in every spare moment of the past three days. Pulling out a stack of envelopes from under the table, already printed with the names and addresses of the travel agents to which they were to be dispatched, she continued with the tedious, repetitive task, pausing occasionally to answer the telephone.

'Darling, I'm so sorry to have left you on your own all this time. Have you coped?'

Tamsin looked up, smothering her immediate smile of amusement as the reservations supervisor made her entrance into the room, followed by a tall girl in her early twenties. Slim, perfectly groomed, her hair tinted a subtle light golden brown, fake eyelashes enhancing the large, honey-coloured eyes, it was impossible to gauge Simone's age, though Tamsin suspected she was somewhere in her fifties.

'Off you go for lunch now, darling. And take a coat because it's beginning to rain.'

'Yes, right. I will.' Lips twitching, Tamsin moved to the door and hesitated, debating whether to mention the air-hostess's request to block off a seat. Deciding it might be more diplomatic not to, she murmured instead, 'I've finished the ticket summary. Shall I drop it off in Accounts?'

'Would you? Thank you, darling.'

Nodding, Tamsin picked up the sheet of paper and envelope from her desk and disappeared out of the door. Only then did she begin to grin. She had been completely disconcerted initially when the reservations supervisor showered her with the endearment but had quickly realized that everyone in the airport was similarly favoured. The notable exception, to Tamsin's secret disappointment, being Jordan.

After depositing the ticket summary in the accounts office, she collected her blue raincoat from the cloakroom, almost colliding with a burly, green-overalled figure as she emerged.

'Hi, Mike.'

'Has darling let you out for lunch?' He grinned at her wickedly. 'I'll just take these off and catch you up.' He disappeared through a door to the left and Tamsin sauntered slowly down the corridor and out of the building, turning up her coat collar against the drizzling rain.

She'd taken a liking to the good-natured, cheerful chief engineer from her first day when, discovering her looking a little lost in the terminal, he'd steered her in the direction of the staff canteen, tucked away behind the public cafeteria.

'Thanks for babysitting last night,' he murmured as he joined her. 'Julie and I really appreciated it.'

'I enjoyed it,' Tamsin admitted honestly. She had been completely entranced by the engineer's beguiling four-year-old twin sons.

'You were a big hit,' he teased her as the terminal doors swung open before them. 'It's your weekend off coming up, isn't it?' As she nodded, he continued, 'Julie was wondering if you'd like to come to lunch on Saturday.'

'I'd love to. Thank you.' She'd felt an instant liking for Mike's clearly adored wife, pregnant with their third child, hoped that their acquaintance would grow into friendship, and the invitation suggested that the sentiment was mutual. The knowledge gave her a warm glow.

It wasn't until that second that she realized how much Jordan had damaged her self-confidence, her sense of worth, made her doubt her ability to be liked, loved simply for herself. Thank God, she thought fervently, that she had resisted him, hadn't fallen into the trap of kidding herself that somehow she would make herself indispensable not just in his bed but in his life.

'Thanks,' she murmured absently as Mike held open the door of the canteen and they joined the queue in front of the serving hatch.

With an air of virtue, Mike selected a salad and then, weakening, added a large quantity of chips to the plate. 'Don't tell Julie.' He winked at Tamsin as they carried their trays over to a vacant table.

As they ate their meals, he kept her entertained with his seemingly endless supply of humorous anecdotes.

'I don't believe a word of it,' Tamsin said, laughing at one particularly outrageous story, the smile stiffening on her lips as over Mike's shoulder she saw Jordan sitting at a table on his own, his eyes like ice directed towards her and her companion. To her intense irritation, Tamsin felt herself flushing.

Mike, watching her, flicked a glance over his shoulder and grinned. 'Not you, too?'

'Pardon?' she muttered, her muscles contracting painfully as she saw Jordan's expression alter instantly as Sara Lyne joined him at his table.

'Crush on the boss.' Mike's voice was teasing. 'It's like an epidemic running through the female population on the airfield. I can't understand what all you women see in him—good-looking, successful swine.'

Tamsin concentrated on her plate, forcing herself to swallow a mouthful of vegetables.

'Actually,' Mike added, 'he's a good bloke and certainly revived Lyne Air. Morale was pretty low before he appeared on the scene.' He paused. 'I had my doubts about him to start with,' he admitted. 'I wondered if he was just investing in the company as some sort of tax dodge. But he's really turned it around.'

As she heard the respect in Mike's voice, Tamsin could do nothing to stop the swell of pride, pride, she reminded herself forcefully, that she had no right to feel. She flicked a quick glance over towards Jordan, moving over the lines of the strong, assured face, his eyes dark and intense as they concentrated on the woman opposite him.

Business. They're just discussing business. The pain inside her was so intense she almost cried out. I want him to be mine. I want the right to be proud of him, to be not just his lover but his best friend. I want to have his children. To shower them with the love *he* never had as a boy. I want to have with him what Mike and Julie have together....

'Hey, Tamsin, are you all right?' Mike suddenly reached over towards her and touched her gently on the shoulder. 'You've gone as white as a sheet.'

'Yes, I'm fine,' she said quickly, trying to clear her swimming head, the nausea gripping her throat. 'It's just a bit warm in here,' she mumbled, appalled at the intensity of the emotions that had exploded inside her.

'Another cup of tea?'

'I think I'd better make a move, actually.' Tamsin began to rise to her feet. She desperately needed some fresh air, to be on her own for a few minutes. 'Karen's taking half a lieu day and I'm minding the reception desk for her this afternoon.'

'A real jack of all trades.' Mike grinned. 'Don't you get confused, not knowing from one day to another what you'll be doing?'

'My first week passed in a total blur,' Tamsin confessed. 'But it's not so bad now I'm beginning to find my way around a bit.'

And, she suddenly realized, she was loving her new job. Far from being a general dogsbody as she'd feared or being treated like a raw recruit, the operations and reservations staff, under increasing pressure preparing for the change-over, had been grateful for her varied airline experience, glad she didn't need constant supervision.

Having worked for a large, impersonal airline for the past years, she found it a pleasant contrast, too, to be part of a tightly knit organization, where all the staff were on easy, friendly terms, where there were no strong demarcation lines between each department.

'Think you'll stay, then?' Mike teased.

'I think so,' she said, grinning back. 'See you.' She began to weave her way through the tables to the door and then stopped, having the sensation of being watched. As she flicked a quick glance back over her shoulder, her gaze passed over the crowd of heads and locked into Jordan's for a brief, imperceptible second. Then quickly, she looked away and headed on out into the terminal.

Would she stay on at Lyne Air, always supposing that she was offered a permanent position at the end of the season? She frowned uneasily. Wasn't half the attraction of the job the bitter-sweet torture of seeing Jordan every day, maintaining some sort of contact with him, if only within a strictly working environment?

The furrows on her forehead deepened. Jordan wouldn't keep a hands-on presence at the airport indefinitely. Once everything was running to his satisfaction, he would probably appoint a manager, move on to his next venture. Her stomach muscles clenched. It was hell seeing him every day... but not doing so was going to be even worse.

The drizzle had changed to rain when she emerged from the terminal and she hurried swiftly back to the administration block, entering by the staff door at the rear. Hanging up her coat, she collected a box of envelopes and timetables from the reservations office and went to relieve the receptionist.

She spent the afternoon manning the switchboard, answering some general enquiries herself, re-routing others to the appropriate departments and completing the mail shot. Sealing the last envelope with relief, she stretched her arms above her head and glanced at the wall clock, surprised to discover it was five o'clock.

'Tamsin?'

She started as the disembodied deep voice came over the intercom. She'd forgotten that the reception desk was linked to Jordan's office.

'Yes?'

'I'd like to see you in my office. Now, please.'

'Yes, sir!' she muttered drily to herself, but her eyes darkened with a flicker of apprehension. There had been an ominous note in Jordan's voice that didn't bode well. She racked her brains to think of something she had done that day to earn his censure but came up a blank. Oh, well, she thought resignedly, there was only one way to find out.

She re-routed all incoming calls through to the operations room, which would be manned until the airport closed, and made her way down the corridor to Jordan's office. She tapped lightly on the door, pushing it open as she heard his response, surprised to find Simone also in occupation, seated in front of Jordan's desk.

Jordan was on the telephone, his chair swivelled away from the desk, enabling him to stretch out his long legs. Frowning at her, he indicated that she should take a seat. She exchanged quick glances with Simone but the expression on the supervisor's face indicated that she was equally perplexed by their joint summons.

'Sara and I will look forward to it.'

The words reverberated in Tamsin's head as she sat down in the hard-backed chair drawn up beside Simone's. *Sara and I.* A couple. Her muscles constricting, she stared out of the window, forcing her attention back to Jordan as she heard the click of the receiver being replaced.

He had removed the jacket of his dark suit, and the cuffs of his brilliant white shirt were folded back on the tanned, muscular forearms.

'Did you make a booking for a Mr. Ian Robinson this morning, travelling on the 1530 Guernsey this afternoon?' he addressed Tamsin without preamble. 'Ticket on departure?'

Startled, she looked at him blankly for a second and then frowned. 'No, I don't think so,' she said hesitantly and then added more positively, 'No, I'm sure I didn't.' The only booking for a Channel Island flight she'd made that morning had been for a couple travelling to Jersey the following week.

Picking up a sheet of printed paper from his desk, Jordan studied it for a second and then raised his eyes. 'There was one no-show on the flight this afternoon. Mr. Ian Robinson.'

Tamsin gazed back at him, a tiny, uneasy suspicion beginning to form in her head.

'Which was quite fortunate for the staff passenger travelling sub load.' Jordan paused. 'I checked out Ian Robinson and it appears that he either gave a false address and telephone number or...' He left the words unsaid, raising his eyebrows.

'I didn't make the booking, Jordan,' Tamsin said quietly.

He surveyed her for one long minute and then handed her the sheet of printed paper. 'The booking was made in your sign!'

She flinched from the anger in his eyes and glanced down at the paper. It was impossible. She had refused to make a fictitious booking. She groaned inwardly. She hadn't switched off her VDU when she'd departed for lunch; it had still been operational in her sign.

She could feel Simone's eyes on her and, flicking her a quick glance, saw the tension on the other woman's face. Doubtlessly, the air-hostess had returned to the office when she'd been at lunch and Simone had carried our her request, automatically using the VDU already in operation. But it was all supposition; she had no real proof.

She met Simone's eyes again. And even if she had proof, she wasn't sure she would want to proffer it to Jordan under the circumstances. Sensing Jordan's gaze on her, she looked back at him squarely.

'Blocking off seats for staff might have been acceptable where you worked before, but at Lyne Air it is grounds for dismissal,' he said curtly.

Tamsin's small jaw clenched. He was going to sack her! Her eyes blazed into his. Damn it, she wasn't going to deny it again. If he didn't believe her, seriously thought she had so little integrity as to do what he had implied, he could go boil his head.

'Um actually, Jordan . . .' Simone's hesitant, unsteady voice broke the silence, but before she could continue, Jordan held up a restraining hand.

'However, in view of the fact that you have only been here three weeks, I'm prepared to let you off with a verbal caution this time.'

Tamsin looked back at him frigidly. What was she supposed to do? Fall to her knees in gratitude for his mercy?

'But if I ever discover you or any other member of staff cheating the airline in this way again, I will have absolutely no compunction in dismissing them. Is that understood?'

'Yes.' Tamsin forced the word out through gritted teeth.

Jordan swivelled his chair. 'Simone, perhaps you could make that quite clear to the rest of your staff? Read them the Riot Act?'

She nodded, and then in unison she and Tamsin rose to their feet and made for the door. Shaking with suppressed anger, Tamsin immediately headed for the cloakroom. She just wanted to get out of this lousy dump as soon as she could.

'Tamsin.' Simone caught up with her as she was shrugging on her coat. 'Thank you,' she said simply.

Wordlessly, Tamsin faced her, read the silent message in the large honey eyes and felt some of her anger draining away.

'I'd better rush or I'll miss my bus,' she said awkwardly and started for the door. She paused for a second and smiled back over her shoulder, and saw the relief on the other woman's face.

'See you tomorrow, darling.'

She couldn't be angry at Simone, Tamsin mused wryly as she left the building. And she was convinced that if it had come to the crunch, the supervisor would have owned up. But as for Jordan!

She kicked at a pebble savagely with her shoe as she cut across the gravelled car park to the road and came to an abrupt halt, cursing under her breath as she saw the tail-end of a bus disappearing into the distance.

Wonderful. That was all she needed, to miss her bus. Thanks a bunch, Jordan. And to add insult to injury, it was beginning to rain again.

She'd walk, she decided quickly. In fact, she'd welcome the physical exertion, a chance to expend the explosion of energy that had been ignited by anger. She began to march rapidly down the road, her pace gradually easing off as she began to calm down and think more rationally.

Why, today of all days, had Jordan suddenly decided to run a check on the passengers failing to join a flight? And why had he thought it necessary to reprimand her in front of Simone? But most puzzling was why, if he genuinely believed she had been responsible for the fictitious booking, he had let her off so lightly.

She came to an abrupt halt. Because Jordan knew damn well she hadn't made that booking. Otherwise she would be clearing her locker by now, of that she was certain!

She'd been set up! Jordan must have suspected that Simone was in the habit of blocking off seats for staff. And he had used Tamsin as a scapegoat in some tactical plan to warn Simone of the consequences if she continued with the practice. She frowned. But that simply didn't make sense. Jordan wouldn't shy away from a confrontation, however unpleasant, so why didn't he tackle Simone directly? Why the subterfuge? Her mouth tightened. And whatever his damn motive, he'd had no right to use her....

Lost in thought, it took a second for her to register the silver grey sports car drawing up beside her. At the same time, she realized that she was drenched, water trickling unpleasantly down her neck, inside the collar of her coat.

The passenger door swung open towards her.

'Get in,' Jordan muttered tersely.

Pride warred momentarily with common sense and then she gave in, slithering into the passenger seat.

'What's happened to your car?' he demanded, glancing over his shoulder before rejoining the traffic.

'I haven't got a car at the moment,' she snapped back. Didn't he even know that about her? 'I've been using public transport or cycling. But my bike had a puncture this morning.'

She was suddenly conscious of the faint lingering scent of expensive women's perfume. At the same time, her eyes alighted on the square of pink silk folded on top of the dashboard, instantly imagining the scarf against Sara Lyne's dark hair.

'What a perfectly ghastly colour,' she murmured sweetly under her breath.

'You won't be able to rely on buses when you start shift work next week. Or cycle if it's pouring rain.' Jordan flicked her a disparaging glance. 'A drowned rat on the check-in desk first thing in the morning is hardly going to enhance Lyne Air's image.'

Slowly and deliberately, Tamsin squeezed a lock of her sodden hair, watching with childish satisfaction as water splattered over the immaculate leather upholstery.

'Actually, Mike knows someone who's selling their car and he's going to check it over for me this weekend before I make an offer.'

'I see.'

Tamsin's eyes jerked to his face. There had been a wealth of meaning in those two short, clipped words. She saw a muscle tighten along his jaw, could feel the anger radiating from his body. What on earth did *he* have to be angry about?

'I assume that you're aware that Mike Reynolds is married with two small sons? That his wife is expecting another child?'

'What?' Tamsin's eyes widened incredulously as she heard the cold censure in his voice. 'I don't believe this. You think I'm having some torrid affair—' her voice shook with laughter, '—just because I've had lunch in the canteen with Mike a few times—'

'I saw you in his car outside the Red Lion last night,' Jordan intervened brusquely.

'For God's sake, Jordan...' The laughter died on her lips. He was serious! 'Mike was only—' She stopped herself quickly. She didn't need to explain anything to Jordan. Was damned if she was going to tell him that Mike had stopped off at the Red Lion last night as he was driving her home after babysitting, to buy a packet of crisps for which Julie had suddenly announced a craving.

She felt a renewed surge of anger. She liked Mike, had looked forward to getting to know Julie and the twins better, becoming a family friend. And Jordan's sordid insinuations had sullied everything.

'Mike is a colleague,' she suddenly flared. 'I like him. But you can't understand that, can you? Can't understand that a man and woman can just be platonic friends. You have to judge everyone by your own standards.'

'So you and Mike are just friends, hmm?' Jordan taunted. 'Like you and Tom?'

'Oh, go to hell!' She glared at him. 'My private life is none of your damn business.' Turning her head, she stared frigidly through the window, reaching for the door handle the moment the car drew up in front of the small semi-detached house she was currently sharing.

* * *

Tamsin lifted one small boy and then the second off the six-seater rocking-horse and then jogtrotted after them as they scampered across the enclosed children's playground to the swings.

'Me first,' two voices demanded in unison, two identical, small freckled faces gazing up at her hopefully.

Having discovered that this constant plea was ignored by Mike and Julie, Tamsin followed suit and indiscriminately strapped the nearer of the twins into the swing and then the second. Pushing them alternatively, she listened to their squeals of delight with a grin.

She was glad she hadn't backed out of Mike and Julie's invitation to lunch, glad she had simply ignored Jordan's insinuations, refused to let him spoil everything after all.

'Higher,' either Simon or Timmy, she wasn't sure which, demanded vociferously.

'Please,' reproved his identical sibling.

Tamsin obeyed dutifully. The change-over had gone like clockwork the day before but then, she thought drily, what else would have been expected with Jordan at the helm? Even the Channel Island weather, which had been erratic at the start of the week, causing delays, hadn't dared defy him, and all the Lyne Air scheduled flights had departed on time to the second.

She glanced at her watch, amazed to see how quickly the afternoon had sped by with her two small entertaining, energetic companions. She smiled. Her offer to take the twins to the nearby park for the afternoon had been greeted by enthusiasm by both the small boys and with appreciation by their parents.

'The bliss of having a couple of hours alone with Mike!' Julie had whispered with a grin as she'd departed.

'One last push,' Tamsin announced firmly, 'and then it's time to go home and have tea.' They protested automatically but acquiesced obediently as she unstrapped them both, sliding their small hands into hers as they made the short homeward journey.

Julie immediately invited her to share tea with them, but Tamsin, noting how weary her hostess looked, declined gracefully and with genuine regret, to howls of disappointment from the twins.

'We wanted to play monsters again,' they wailed, following her out the front door.

'Come and help me get Tamsin's bike from the back.' Mike swiftly distracted them both, herding them around the side of the house, returning a few moments later with the push-bike.

'Thanks.' Tamsin grabbed hold of the handlebars, pushing the bike down the front path onto the road before mounting it. The whole family, including an elderly black Labrador and a disdainful tabby cat, gathered to see her off, the twins waving madly until she disappeared from view.

Engulfed in a mood of warm contentment, Tamsin hummed under her breath as she pedalled the short distance homewards along the quiet side-roads. After locking her bike safely up in the garage, she entered the front door and her mood was instantly dispelled, the contrast between the noisy, cheerful household she'd just left and the silence and emptiness now surrounding her hitting her forcefully.

She made her way into the kitchen, switched on the kettle and sat down and reviewed the long evening ahead, the equally barren day tomorrow. Her flatmate was on early shift tomorrow but would doubtlessly be spending the remainder of the day with her fiancé as she did every free moment.

Restlessly, Tamsin rose to her feet and paced the kitchen. She was lonely, she registered with shock. Solitude in the shared flat in Croydon had been a luxury, never an enforced state.

She slumped back in a chair again. She was missing Tom, she thought with a sigh. He had been so much a part of her life over the past few years. Why couldn't she have cared for him in the same way he did her? she thought for the millionth time. He was considerate, kind, fun to be with, attractive... Her heart gave a painful thud. But he wasn't Jordan....

She shuddered, fear gripping her, her eyes darkening with sudden panic. Surely she wasn't going to spend the rest of her life wanting the unattainable, something that would never be hers....

She slammed the table with her palm. One thing she was not going to do was spend the evening moping about Jordan Keston. She'd walk down to the local sports centre and see what courses were on offer, take up a new activity. She forced her lips into a grin. Wasn't that the standard agony aunt recommendation—join new clubs, find new interests, meet new people?

The peal of the doorbell made her jolt, and eyes still reflective, she went to answer it, her stomach somersaulting at the sight of Jordan, formally dressed in a dark suit, standing on the doorstep.

His appearance was so totally unexpected that she had no time to compose herself, all her senses exploding into life. Her eyes feasted on the strong, assured lines of his face, her sense of smell teased by the faint, elusive scent of soap, aftershave and male skin. Swiftly, she thrust her hands into the pockets of her jeans, aching to reach out and touch him. She could almost feel the hard muscles of his shoulders beneath her damp palms.

'Your telephone is out of order,' he drawled.

'Thank you for sharing that with me,' she retorted caustically. He'd come here just to tell her that? Her heart was hammering so loudly beneath her ribcage she was sure he must hear it.

'I have reported it,' he continued. 'Have you eaten this evening?'

She was thrown completely off balance by the unexpected change of direction. 'No... not yet.'

'Good.' He surveyed her blue T-shirt and grass-stained jeans and glanced at his watch. 'Can you be ready in fifteen minutes?'

What? 'I'm sorry if I'm being a little obtuse, Jordan,' she murmured coolly, 'but I think I'm missing something here.'

'I've arranged to have dinner tonight with the chairman of Simpson Travel and his wife. Sara was accompanying me but unfortunately she's suddenly come down with a migraine and it's a little late to cancel at this stage.'

'Oh, I see.' Tamsin smiled sweetly. 'And I'm first reserve?'

He looked back at her expressionlessly. 'Whatever is discussed tonight will be strictly confidential.'

She searched his face, trying to ignore the tiny swell of pleasure that the implication of his words gave her.

'So suddenly I'm to be trusted?' she said acidly. 'Odd, considering that a few days ago, you virtually accused me of lying to you, cheating the airline.' Her eyes flashed.

'You knew damn well I hadn't blocked that seat off even though it was in my sign. You used me like a pawn.'

'Yes,' he agreed simply.

'Yes?' she flared. 'That's it? Yes. No explanation or apology?'

'I had my reasons.'

'Oh, that's just great!' she snorted.

Jordan glanced at his watch again. 'Ten minutes.'

Her eyes locked into his rebelliously. Didn't it even occur to him that she might have other plans for the evening?

'It's a business dinner, Tamsin. That's all,' he said with the aggravating patience of an adult trying to soothe a belligerent child. 'Book it down as overtime,' he added drily.

'Oh, what the hell,' she muttered and, whisking away, tore up the stairs. She dashed into the bathroom and came to a halt. Damn it! She wasn't going to go rushing round like a lunatic. She was doing Jordan a favour, heaven knows why, and he could just wait until she was ready.

She ran warm water into the basin and opened the cabinet above it to retrieve a new bar of soap, accidentally knocking a bottle, which tumbled into the basin. She started to fish it out and froze, staring mesmerized at the crimson water engulfing her hand. Her head spinning, she jerked herself away from the basin, propelled herself towards the door and out onto the landing, desperately trying to reach her bedroom before the grey mist engulfed her completely.

'You're all right, sweetheart. Don't try and lift your head. Just lie still.'

She must be dreaming, Tamsin mused dazedly as she looked up into concerned dark blue eyes, the endearment still echoing in her ears. Her eyelids flickered down again. Slowly, she became aware of the hard tiled floor beneath her head, the carpet beneath her outstretched legs. Her eyes flew open as recollection dawned. Oh, God, not again...would that nightmare ever leave her?

'Can you sit up?'

'Yes,' she muttered, instantly conscious of the gentle hands on her shoulders as Jordan eased her into a sitting position. She was on the threshold of the bathroom, the lower half of her body protruding onto the carpeted landing. She must have just managed to tug open the door before—

'I broke a bottle in the basin and cut my hand,' she said, shuddering convulsively. She refused to look at Jordan, couldn't bear to see the derision on his face. 'C-could you empty the basin...please...and give me a plaster...?' Her head was pounding, waves of nausea flowing over her.

Wordlessly, Jordan rose to his feet and edged past her. She heard the gurgle of water.

'Tamsin.' He squatted down beside her again.

Slowly, she turned her head towards him, her face ashen.

'You didn't cut yourself,' he said quietly. 'The bottle was plastic. Henna shampoo.'

'Oh, God!' she croaked, burying her face in her hands. She'd fainted over a bottle of shampoo! She could feel the well of hysteria rising up inside her, began to laugh...

'Stop that!'

She jerked her head up as she heard the thunderous voice and then, before she had time to register what was happening, was being scooped up effortlessly into Jordan's arms and carried along the landing.

'Which room?'

'Second one,' she mumbled.

Nudging the door open with his shoulder, he carried her across the patterned carpet and laid her gently down on the bed, pulling up the lilac duvet around her.

'I'm calling the doctor. I'll use the car phone.'

'No,' Tamsin protested.

'You've a whacking great bruise on your temple where you hit the door and might well be concussed,' he informed her in a tone that brooked no argument, then he disappeared from the room.

Defeatedly, Tamsin sank back onto the pillow and waited for his return. It was so easy just to give in somehow, so easy to let Jordan take charge.

'Your business dinner...' she muttered as he strode back through the door. 'You'll be late.'

'I've called the restaurant and left a message for the Simpsons.'

'I'm sorry,' she mumbled.

'It was only a dinner, Tamsin,' he said quietly and sat down on the edge of the bed. 'A lot of people have phobias. Fear of enclosed spaces, heights, flying.'

She turned her head to look at him. 'Don't patronize me,' she said shortly.

'You need help,' he continued as if she hadn't spoken. 'Professional help. Therapy.'

Her jaw tightened. 'I had all that when—' She slammed her mouth shut, averting her face.

'When what, Tamsin?' he prodded gently.

Slowly, she turned her head back towards him, her eyes locking into his. They were dark, almost black. She could feel her defences crumbling, her resistance being swept away under the intensity of his gaze.

'What happened?' he urged her again.

She swallowed. 'I was fourteen... cycling home from school.' Her large, luminous eyes remained focused steadily on his face. 'I came around a bend in the lane and there was a c-car in the ditch.' She paused and took a deep breath. 'There was a man in the driver's seat. He wasn't wearing a seat-belt and was covered in b-blood. I thought he was dead at first but he was still breathing.' Her voice began to shake. 'I didn't know what to do. There was no other traffic and the nearest house was over half a mile away. I wanted to do something to help him but I didn't even know the most basic first aid....'

Vaguely, she was conscious of the warm, firm fingers curving around her hand.

'In the end, I ran to the nearest house to phone an ambulance.' Her eyes widened with distress. 'I ran when I had a bike. But I just couldn't think straight. I just panicked completely. I felt so helpless, so inadequate....' She licked her dry lips. 'By the time the ambulance arrived, he was d-dead.'

'And you've always blamed yourself?'

'I should have done more... gone for assistance straight away instead of dithering... should have done something more to help him... shouldn't have just left him to... to...'

'You weren't responsible for the accident, Tamsin. And I very much doubt there was anything more you or anyone else could have done.'

She had heard those exact words of reassurance countless times in the past, and yet for the first time, the words spoken in the quiet, assured voice held some degree of comfort.

'I enrolled for a first-aid course shortly afterwards. I never wanted to feel so useless again. One lesson was a little too realistic and that's when I first keeled over and started having nightmares. . . .' She tried to laugh but the sound choked in her throat, came out as a sob.

Strong arms eased her across the bed, and the next moment she was siting on Jordan's lap, cradled against him, her head pressed against his shoulder as the tears streamed down her face.

'It's all right,' his deep voice murmured soothingly against her ear, lean, sensitive fingers stroking her hair.

'I thought I'd finally come to terms with it, put it all behind me,' she mumbled as her sobs slowly subsided. 'I haven't actually fainted for years. Not since . . .' Her voice trailed away.

Jordan's fingers cupped her chin, tilting her face upwards towards his. 'Not since you slugged me on the jaw?' His mouth quirked.

Her own mouth curved in response. 'Well, yes.' Her eyes locked into his and suddenly it was no longer comforting or reassuring being nestled against him, but alarming. She could feel the male strength of his body fusing into hers, feel the warmth of his breath against her upturned face.

'I knew you were going to be trouble the moment I saw you,' he muttered, his voice not quite steady. Slowly, he traced the contour of her cheek with his fingers. Hypnotized, she gazed up at him, tiny goose bumps tingling down her spine. 'You're shivering.' Abruptly, Jordan tipped her gently back onto the bed, covering her with the duvet. 'It's probably delayed shock.'

The only shock was the concern in his voice, the unveiled expression in his dark blue eyes. It had to be a trick of the light.

'Where is that damn doctor?' He suddenly strode to the window and scanned the street. 'If he's not here in a few more minutes, I'm driving you to hospital.'

Tamsin stared at him incredulously. This was Jordan? Pacing agitatedly around the room because she had a bump on the head? She liked it. Oh, she definitely liked it. And it was decidedly worth that throbbing behind her temple. She frowned.

'What?' He quirked a quizzical eyebrow at her and, pulling up a chair beside the bed, folded his long frame into it.

'You,' she said simply. 'A few days ago, you were threatening to fire me for something I hadn't done, more or less accusing me of having an affair with a married man, and now...' She flushed slightly, closing her mouth. She mustn't start reading too much into this situation. Her eyes moved over his face. 'You don't really believe that Mike and I are involved, do you?' she asked quietly.

'No.'

'Then why on earth...?'

He shrugged his broad shoulders dismissively. 'I don't know.'

Tamsin raised her eyebrows in disbelief. Nothing Jordan ever said or did was uncalculated. He was too controlled, always too much in command of himself to act on impulse. She sighed inwardly as she saw the shutters slam down over his eyes, knew it was pointless pursuing the matter. 'So why did you set me up with

Simone? Or is that a state secret, too?' she added caustically.

'I wasn't exactly fair to you,' he admitted.

And accusing her of having an affair with Mike had been fair?

He sighed resignedly. 'I guessed Simone had probably blocked off the seat, suspected she had been doing it for years.'

'So why didn't you simply have it out with her? Why use me?'

'Because I wanted to warn her off but I didn't want to have to sack her,' he said quietly. 'As you were a new, relatively inexperienced staff member, I could simply give you a warning, but I could hardly take an equally lenient line with the supervisor.' He paused. 'Simone and Sam Lyne were lovers for twenty-five years.'

Tamsin stared at him. 'Sam Lyne... Sara's father?'

He nodded. 'Sam confided in me several years ago, made me promise that I would look after Simone should anything happen to him.' His mouth curved wryly. 'Discreetly, of course. And sacking her hardly fell into that category.'

'Twenty-five years,' Tamsin muttered. 'So that's why Simone never married, had children.' Her eyes darkened with compassion. 'How could she accept a situation like that?' God, what a waste of a life. Loving someone who would never be hers. She was appalled and then angry. 'How could he do that to Simone? To his wife? She must have known or at least suspected.'

'No,' Jordan denied. 'She didn't and still doesn't. Of that I'm sure. Nor does Sara.'

Tamsin's fingers picked at the edge of the duvet. Why had Sam Lyne picked Jordan as his confidant? The two

men must have been exceptionally close. Her stomach
muscles knotted together, the stab of pain cutting
through her, making her throbbing head seem insignificant. Through Jordan's relationship with Sara, Sam
Lyne must have come to regard Jordan almost as one
of the family, probably even viewed him as a future son-
in-law.

'Don't make judgements about a man you never even
met,' Jordan said quietly.

'Of course you would side with him,' she flashed back,
glad that he had evidently misinterpreted her expression,
glad, too, that he had given her the opportunity to vent
that rush of irrational, unjustified anger against him.

'Possibly I am a little biased,' he agreed evenly. 'Sam
Lyne was my foster-father until Andrew adopted me.'

For a moment, Tamsin was too stunned to speak and
then everything started to click into place. 'You told me
that you and Sara used to live together.'

'Mmm.' Jordan smiled blandly. 'For four years until
I was ten.'

'You deliberately misled me!'

'Did I?' he murmured innocently.

'You know perfectly well you did!'

He shrugged carelessly. 'I wanted to see your reaction.'

'My reaction?' Tamsin echoed icily. What was she?
A performing poodle?

'Oh, for God's sake, Tamsin, don't be so dense!' he
suddenly thundered and, leaping to his feet, paced over
to the window.

Tamsin glared at his back. 'Your bedside manner
needs attention.'

Abruptly, he swung round to face her. 'I wanted to make you jealous.'

Tamsin's eyes flew to his face. There was a look of vulnerability, of hesitancy, she had never witnessed before. If it wasn't so totally ludicrous, she would have said that Jordan Keston actually looked nervous. Her pulse rate suddenly doubled.

'Why?' she said unsteadily. 'Why did you want to make me jealous?'

A muscle flickered along the line of the hard, uncompromising jaw. 'Why the hell do you think?' he muttered gruffly, his voice so low that she had to strain her ears to hear it. 'Because...oh, damn it!' he exploded as the doorbell chimed through the house, and spinning on his heel, he turned towards the door.

'Jordan...' Tamsin called after him with frustration but her words fell into empty space. Slumping back on the pillow, she stared up at the ceiling with wide, confused eyes. 'Come in,' she muttered a few moments later in response to the tap on the door and forced herself to smile at the brisk, middle-aged man who entered the room.

Absently, she answered his questions as he examined her. What had Jordan been about to say? Don't start letting your imagination run riot, she ordered herself, or be fooled by that earlier show of concern and gentleness. After all, he could hardly have left her lying on the floor....

Conscious that the doctor was snapping his bag shut, she forced herself to concentrate on the tail-end of his words.

'...but I think it would be advisable to have an X-ray just to be on the safe side.'

She nodded. 'Thank you, Dr. Green,' she murmured and then frowned. An X-ray... 'Um, there's something else. I think it's probably a false alarm but there's just a faint chance...' She took a deep breath.

CHAPTER EIGHT

'ARE you warm enough?' Jordan enquired courteously, his eyes never straying from the road. 'Would you like the heater turned up?'

'No, thank you. I'm fine,' Tamsin returned with equal politeness. Cautiously, she slid him a sideways glance. The strong, masculine features were impassive but the flicker of a muscle along the line of his hard jaw, the knuckles of his lean hands gripping the steering wheel betrayed his tension.

She focused her gaze back out the window but every inch of her was aware of the man by her side, alert to his slightest movement. The silence was becoming unendurable.

'This really is a waste of time.' Her voice was unnatural, too high-pitched.

'You heard the doctor,' Jordan returned quietly. 'The X-ray is merely a precaution.'

'Well, I'm sure it's unnecessary. I feel perfectly all right,' she lied. Her head was thudding but whether it was from the knock on her temple or caused by the tension in the car she didn't know. She could feel the familiar frustration swirling up inside her as she shot him another sideways glance. He'd withdrawn away from her again. The man who had sat cradling her in his arms such a short time ago had been transformed into this courteous but remote stranger.

Her eyes widened with horror as she felt the nausea welling up in her throat. 'Jordan...could you stop the car, p-please?' she mumbled desperately, terrified of committing the ultimate humiliation in front of him.

As the car jerked to a halt, she wrenched open the door, stumbling onto the verge. She gulped air into her lungs and slowly felt the wave of sickness receding.

'Feel better?'

'Yes,' she mumbled, feeling the touch of Jordan's hand on her shoulder. Shakily, she turned round to face him.

He looked down at her and then pulled her wordlessly into the circle of his arms. Her head fell against his chest, her eyes closing. She felt so safe, enveloped in a secure, protective cocoon, then gave a little protesting mew as she felt his hold slacken.

'The sooner you get to hospital the better,' Jordan muttered gruffly and then, catching her totally unawares, crushed her against him. 'Oh, God, if anything should ever happen to you...'

Slowly and disbelievingly, Tamsin raised her eyes to his face. Had she heard him correctly? The expression in the dark blue eyes made her draw in her breath. Perhaps she really was concussed, she thought wildly.

'If anything ever happened to me...' she prompted unsteadily.

His mouth quirked. 'Your mother would doubtlessly hold me responsible and have me shot at dawn,' he said carelessly.

Tamsin froze as she saw the veil dropping over his eyes, the male features forming into a bland mask. She was so sick of this, just couldn't deal with this constant emotional see-saw any longer.

'Why do you do this to me every time?' The words tore from her throat before she even had time to think. 'Make me believe you care and then just switch off, push me away?' Her voice shook. 'It's cruel, Jordan. Sadistic.' She wheeled away from him.

'Tamsin!' He snaked out a hand and spun her back towards him. 'Is that what you want?' he demanded urgently. 'Me to care about you?'

Oh, no, she wasn't going to fall into that little trap, make herself wide open and vulnerable, give him further ammunition with which to taunt her in the future.

'Care?' She laughed brittlely. 'You don't know the meaning of the word, Jordan. You're incapable of caring, of any real depth of feeling for anyone.' She wrenched her hand from his grasp. Her head was thudding so much she could hardly think straight. 'I pity any woman who ever falls in love with you because it would be like trying to love a brick wall. Maybe your early childhood stunted your emotional development but...'

She stopped, appalled, her eyes dark with shame and self-disgust. She was behaving like a thwarted child, striking out because she couldn't have what she wanted. And that last gibe about his childhood had been unforgivable. 'Jordan, I'm sorry,' she muttered huskily.

His face was unreadable, a granite mask. His eyes sweeping over her reflected nothing but indifference. Her words had hardly penetrated, let alone wounded him, she realized slowly. You had to care about someone before they could hurt you, she acknowledged. She turned back towards the car and this time Jordan made no effort to restrain her.

*　　*　　*

Overnight for observation. Hugging the white hospital gown around her, Tamsin scrambled into bed under the watchful eye of the uniformed figure. It had never occurred to her that she might actually be admitted to the hospital, hadn't even thought about bringing an overnight case.

The middle-aged nurse gave her a brisk smile. 'Your boyfriend's waiting outside to say goodbye. Two minutes and that's all,' she added firmly, moving off down the ward.

Tamsin looked across to the door and saw the lean figure striding towards her. Boyfriend? she thought drily. Wrong on both counts. Her lips twitched despite herself. Jordan was hardly a boy! Her smile faded. And friend would be about the last word she'd ever use to describe their relationship.

'I didn't expect you to wait,' she greeted Jordan coolly as he reached the bed. She'd assumed he'd left the hospital when she'd been taken up to the ward, relieved that he'd expended his duty, that she was no longer his responsibility.

He shrugged, his expression indifferent. 'I'll come and collect you in the morning,' he informed her crisply.

'You needn't bother,' she returned swiftly. 'I'm perfectly capable of catching a bus.' She feigned a yawn. 'And if you don't mind, I really am very tired.'

She saw his mouth tighten. 'Good night, Tamsin.'

Her eyes dark with misery, she watched him stride back across the ward, wanting desperately to call him back. She hadn't even thanked him for bringing her to hospital.

Until her outburst, Jordan had been kind, considerate, gentle. Why couldn't she have settled for that?

Why had she to spoil everything by wanting more? Squeezing her eyes shut, she buried her face in the pillow.

Slipping the hospital gown back on after her bath, Tamsin pulled the borrowed comb through her long, tousled hair and pulled a wry face as she inspected herself in the mirror above the basin.

'You're no thing of beauty this morning,' she informed the reflected image kindly. The livid bruise on her temple stood out luridly against her ashen skin and there were dark shadows under her eyes. But although she could have quite easily crawled back into bed for the next twenty-four hours, the throbbing in her head had mercifully stopped.

Tightening the robe around her slim figure, she padded back to the ward, scrambling in between the sheets of her bed just as the doctor began his morning rounds.

He smiled at her briskly from the foot of her bed. 'How are you feeling today?'

'Much better,' she said, smiling back at the white-coated figure. She thought it was the same doctor who had admitted her yesterday but couldn't be sure. Everything about the preceding evening had assumed a dreamlike quality.

'No more dizziness?' He gestured to the attendant nurse to pull the screens around the bed. 'Good,' he murmured with satisfaction after his brief examination and then picked up the folder he had deposited on the chair and flicked through it. He raised his head. 'We've had the result of your test back from the lab,' he said quietly. 'It's positive.'

Tamsin stared at him numbly. 'You mean I'm pregnant?' She shook her head. 'I don't believe it...I didn't think for one moment that I really could be...I've always been erratic and I thought with the stress of a new job...' And she'd been taking a contraceptive. She closed her eyes. She'd had a stomach upset that preceding week.... It had never occurred to her... Her eyes opened. 'Are you sure? There couldn't be some mistake?'

'No,' the doctor said quietly.

She saw the concern in his eyes, realized that he must be aware of her single status and uncertain of how welcome was the news.

Welcome? Jordan's baby? She was going to have Jordan's baby! She hadn't even dared to contemplate it until now, terrified of the disappointment. She began to grin inanely, her eyes glowing.

'Congratulations.' The doctor smiled with evident relief. 'Make an appointment to see your local GP.'

She nodded, hardly aware of his departure, still gripped by euphoria. She wanted to shout out her news to the world. She felt different. Did she look different? Jordan's baby. A part of him that would always belong to her. Dazedly, she registered the figure by her bed.

'Sorry?'

The young student nurse grinned. 'Your boyfriend's brought a change of clothes in for you.' She placed a small canvas bag on the locker. 'He's waiting in the day-room.'

'Thanks.' Tamsin beamed as the nurse disappeared. Not her boyfriend. But the father of her child. She opened the bag and inspected the contents. Jordan had presumably been round to the house and asked her flatmate for the clean underwear and toiletries. Humming, she began to dress and suddenly laughed out loud. Jordan's child within her body.

'Oh, my God! I'm going to have a baby!' She slumped down onto the bed. She was pregnant. Unmarried. Not in any long-term, committed relationship. She was going to have a child, be solely responsible for its welfare, up-bringing. She could feel beads of perspiration forming on her brow, panic twisting her body, as reality, ration-ality, the sheer practicalities of what lay ahead crashed through the euphoria.

But there was one thing of which she was certain. She wanted this child, wanted it more than anything in the world. And she would manage. Other women brought up children single-handedly, coped, and so would she.

She rose to her feet. And now somehow she had to face Jordan. She bit her lip.

'Nearly ready?' A nurse popped her head around the curtain. 'Your boyfriend has had to rush off but he's arranged a taxi for you.'

Tamsin nodded, pretending to be busy fastening the zip of her small case. Jordan couldn't be bothered to wait even a few minutes for her, had dutifully deposited her clothes and rushed off. The stab of pain that tore through her was so intense that she almost cried out. He had handed her over to a taxi as if she were an unwanted parcel. Well, she was glad, relieved that she wouldn't have to face him today after all....

'Hey, are you all right?' the nurse enquired.

'I'm fine,' Tamsin said brightly and burst into tears.

'This is a final check-in call for Lyne Air flight 326 to Jersey and Guernsey. Would all passengers not yet in possession of a boarding card for this service, please attend the check-in desk in the main hall?'

Releasing the button on the Tannoy, Tamsin's eyes flicked to the wall clock above it. She would close the flight in a few more minutes and then hand over to the late shift. And tomorrow, she thought thankfully, she had a day off, the first one in the past fortnight.

There had been the opportunity to work overtime last week and she had grabbed it, conscious now of the need to save every penny from her salary. It was odd how calm she'd felt in the past couple of days, she reflected, and how strangely isolated from the rest of the world.

She smiled at the elderly couple approaching the desk with their suitcases.

'If you'd like to put your cases on the scale?' She glanced down at their ticket to check their destination and then stiffened as she looked up and saw Jordan walking through the automatic glass doors into the terminal. She'd seen little of him since her return to work, had at times wondered if he were deliberately avoiding her. On the few occasions she had encountered him on his own in the corridor in the administration block, he had acknowledged her presence with a brisk nod but made no attempt at conversation.

Quickly, she extracted two destination tags from the pigeon-holes on the desk and tied them around the cases.

'Excuse me, miss. But we're going to Jersey, not Guernsey.'

'Oh, I'm sorry.' Tamsin gave what she hoped was a reassuring, confident smile and swiftly rectified the error. With a sinking heart, she realized that Jordan was standing a few feet away, had doubtlessly witnessed the mistake. The smile still fixed to her face, she pulled the relevant coupon from the ticket and handed it back to the passengers together with their boarding cards and baggage receipts. 'Your flight will be called through gate number two in twenty minutes.'

As the couple moved away, she turned her attention to the fair man who had been queuing behind them.

'I asked for a non-smoking seat and I've just looked at my boarding card and you gave me smoking.'

'I'm sorry, sir.' Unhappily conscious that Jordan was still within earshot, Tamsin reissued the seat number, grateful that the flight wasn't full.

'I did request a window seat.'

'I'm sorry but the only seats left in non-smoking are aisle seats.' Please don't be difficult, not with Jordan watching.

Grumbling under his breath, the man ambled away. Refusing to even glance at Jordan, she bent her head, quickly totalled the figures on the sheet of paper in front of her and picked up the internal telephone to relay the passenger figures and baggage weight to the operations office.

Out of the corner of her eye, she saw Jordan approaching the desk and, replacing the receiver, looked up at him resignedly.

'I'd like to see you in my office when you've finished your shift,' he said quietly and turned away.

Sighing under her breath, she collected up the ticket coupons and placed them in an envelope with the passenger list. Then as soon as her relief arrived, she made her way back from the terminal to the administration block.

'Come in,' Jordan commanded as she knocked at his door. He was standing by the window, his back to her as she entered the office. 'Sit down, Tamsin.'

How did he know it was even her? she wondered as she obeyed. He hadn't even glanced at her.

'What's the matter, Tamsin?' He turned round, his dark blue eyes moving pensively over her face. 'You've been late for three early shifts in the past fortnight.' He moved across the carpet and sat down behind his desk. 'You've made numerous careless errors and seem to be suffering from increasing lapses in concentration. Why, Tamsin?' he demanded evenly.

She stiffened, completely thrown off balance. She had mentally braced herself for a reprimand but not this quiet inquisition. Uneasily, she stared down at the carpet. 'I've already apologized to the senior duty officer,' she said evasively.

'Next time you're late, Tamsin, unless you can offer a legitimate excuse...' He let the unspoken threat hang in the air.

Tamsin bit her lip. Pull your socks up or else. She couldn't afford to lose this job, needed to continue working for as long as she was able.

'Would you like a coffee?'

Startled, she looked up as Jordan rose to his feet. 'No, thank you,' she said swiftly, blanching. Even the thought of it made her feel queasy.

'How crass of me.' Jordan sat down again, stretching out his long legs. 'The smell of coffee, hmm? It affects a lot of pregnant women like that, so I believe.'

Tamsin went rigid. She tried to speak but her lips seemed frozen.

'There's no point in denying it, Tamsin,' Jordan said quietly. 'I found out the morning I came to pick you up at the hospital. The sister had to leave her office while I was there and she left your notes on her desk.'

'And you looked at them?' The colour drained from her face. So that was why he had left without waiting for her. The moment he had discovered she was pregnant, he had just walked out. Pain twisted inside her like a knife. 'You had no damn right—'

'No right to know that you are carrying my child?' he thundered, pushing back his chair. He began to pace jerkily around the room. 'Why the hell didn't you tell me yourself?' He ground to a halt in front of his desk and then cursed as the internal telephone rang.

'Yes?' he bit out as he picked up the receiver. 'Tell him I'll call him back. Tomorrow. And, Jill, I shall be out of the office for the rest of the day.' He slammed down the receiver and looked up. 'We need to talk. Somewhere with no interruptions.'

'I can't see what there's left to talk about,' Tamsin returned huskily. Hell, she was going to burst into tears any minute and breaking down was the last thing she wanted to do in front of Jordan. 'It's my problem and I shall deal with it.'

A muscle tightened along his jaw. 'A problem?' he rasped. 'Is that how you see it? And how many solutions have you considered?' His mouth tightened. 'Abortion?' he lashed.

'No!' she choked. Her eyes wide with shock and disgust, Tamsin dropped her hands protectively to her abdomen. How could he think for a moment that she would even contemplate such a course of action? She began to shudder convulsively.

'I'm sorry. That was unpardonable.'

Slowly, she looked up. Jordan had risen to his feet and was crossing the room towards her. Gently, he laid a hand on her arm and pulled her to her feet.

'Come on,' he said quietly and shepherded her from the room.

'Would you like to get out and walk?' Jordan asked as he drew the car to a halt in the deserted car park of a local beauty spot.

'Yes.' Tamsin nodded. Rolling meadows lay in front of them, stretching down to a river, shimmering under the May sunshine. Calm and therapeutic. Slipping off her uniform jacket, Tamsin slid out of the car.

'The footpath starts by that gate,' Jordan murmured, guiding her towards it.

Tamsin breathed in the fresh, scented air as they walked along in silence, the sun warm on her bare arms. She could feel the tension easing from her body, her muscles beginning to relax. Rounding a bend, they reached a gate and paused, leaning over it, gazing at the view beyond.

'If I hadn't found out, would you have ever told me about the baby?' Jordan finally broke the silence.

'I don't know,' Tamsin said honestly. It was a decision she had been unable to reach, one that had plagued her every waking thought. 'Probably. Eventually.'

Jordan's hands were resting on the top bar of the gate, only inches away from hers. Lean, capable. The temptation to touch them, to draw strength from them was overwhelming. Deliberately, she raised her head and stared reflectively into the distance.

'It's not something I could have kept secret forever anyway,' she added wryly.

'Didn't it occur to you that I might be interested in the fact that you were carrying my child?'

Not your child. Our child. Tamsin's eyes leaped to his face as the words screamed in her head. 'So interested that the second you found out, you fled the hospital!'

'I was angry,' Jordan said quietly. 'Angry because you hadn't told me yourself.'

'But I didn't know myself until then.'

He raised a sceptical dark eyebrow. 'Oh, come on. You must have suspected, had some inkling.' His eyes darkened. 'Or did you just block your mind off to it? Hope it would go away?'

'It?' She rounded on him. 'It's not an it...it's a baby—'

'Our baby,' Jordan muttered gruffly, his voice so low that Tamsin only just managed to decipher the words.

Her eyes jerked to his face, hope surging inside her.

'I won't marry you,' he said evenly, looking down at her.

The hope was expelled as quickly as it had been ignited. 'I don't recall asking you to!' But hadn't some part of her expected him to at least make the gesture? Even though she would have refused.

'It wouldn't work,' he continued quietly. 'We would be getting married for all the wrong reasons.'

'Yes,' she mumbled. A marriage without love. Just like the one his parents had been forced into.

'It wouldn't be fair on anyone,' he continued. 'Not least the child.'

Tamsin bit her lip. Was he comparing her with his mother? Did he seriously think that she would ever walk out on their child? Then unbidden, her thoughts turned to her own mother, enduring her father's infidelity for *her* sake.

'No,' she finally muttered, vaguely conscious that they had turned round and were retracing their steps back along the footpath.

'But that doesn't mean I don't want to be involved,' Jordan said softly. 'And not simply financially. I want to be part of our son's or daughter's life.' He unlocked the car and held the passenger door open for her. 'And I'd like you to come and stay at Swallow Lodge at least until the baby's born.'

She stiffened. 'You want me to give up work? Immediately?' Become totally dependent on him financially. 'And if I refuse?'

He shrugged but the set of his square chin left her in no doubt about the answer.

'I see. You'd terminate my employment,' she said flatly. And as a temporary employee she would have no real recourse if he chose to do so. 'Of course, I appreciate that I would be an embarrassment at the airport once my condition became apparent,' she said bitterly. 'Much more convenient to have me secreted out of the way at Swallow Lodge.' She slithered into her seat and slammed the door shut with all her might.

'Think about it,' Jordan murmured as he joined her. 'Shift work, irregular hours, irregular meals, on your feet for much of the time.'

She didn't answer but was forced to recognize the sense of his words. At the same time, it suddenly occurred to her that he hadn't once questioned the fact that he was the father of her baby. Nor had he demanded to know how she had become pregnant after assuring him that she was on the pill. He hadn't apportioned any blame to her, had accepted and recognized his own responsibility. Her mouth tightened. And was dealing with the situation in his usual calm, rational, unemotional way.

Her hands formed into fists in her lap. And after the baby was born? What then? Her eyes glazed over as the scenario formed in her head. Jordan would provide a house for her, give her a generous allowance. She and the baby would be financially secure for life. She ought to be grateful; countless women would envy her.

And she would spend every day waiting for him to phone, to appear on the doorstep. Except it wouldn't be her he wanted to speak to, to see. And one day, he would come accompanied, introduce the woman by his side as his future wife.

She was going to end up like Simone, spend the rest of her life wanting a man who would never be hers. She would never be free of Jordan. Because of a one-night stand that had meant nothing more to him than sexual gratification, part of her was bound to him forever. Bleakly, she stared out the window as Jordan turned into the familiar road and drew to a halt.

She reached for the door handle and paused. 'I'd be grateful if you wouldn't say anything to my mother or Andrew yet,' she said formally. 'I'd rather wait until after their wedding, when they return from their honeymoon.' It wouldn't be fair to mar her mother's happiness straight away.

'As you wish,' Jordan returned evenly as she scrambled from the car. 'Don't forget your jacket.'

She nodded and, slinging it over her shoulder, walked up the path. She was just about to insert her key in the front door when she heard a woman scream.

She swung round, her eyes opening in horror as she saw the toddler dive out into the road in front of Jordan.

There was the squeal of brakes followed by the sickening thud of metal as the car swerved into a lamppost.

'Oh, my God! Jordan!' As she raced towards the car, she could see him slumped back in his seat. 'Jordan,' she cried out despairingly, wrenching open the driver's door.

His eyes were closed, a line of dark red trickling down the side of his face. She froze. Her nightmare had turned back to reality. Then, adrenalin surged through her, releasing her cramped muscles from their immobility.

'Please be all right, Jordan,' she croaked as, acting on autopilot, she felt for the pulse in his neck. 'I couldn't bear it if...' She sighed her relief as she registered the strong, regular beat. 'I love you so much,' she whispered huskily, hardly aware that she had spoken the words hammering in her brain out loud. Pulling a clean tissue from the pocket of her jacket, she wiped his face gently.

'I think it's only a superficial graze,' a deep voice drawled. Blue eyes flicked open and surveyed her.

'You were bluffing!' Tamsin's face flamed with furious colour as he nonchalantly swung himself out of the car and stood towering over her. 'How could you do that to me? You lousy, stinking—'

'And by the way, I love you, too.'

'...rotten bastard...what?' Tamsin's stomach lurched. She can't have heard correctly. Must have misheard him. Blood pounding in her ears, Tamsin searched his face with wide, uncertain eyes. If this was another of his games... She drew in a short, shallow breath as she saw the expression in his eyes, her head beginning to swim.

'I love you, Tamsin... I want to marry you.'

As she heard the catch in his voice, saw the look of naked vulnerability in his eyes, any remaining doubts vanished. 'You really love me?' she said weakly, her eyes glowing.

'More than anything in the world,' he muttered gruffly and pulled her gently into his arms. 'I fell in love with you that first summer.'

She tilted her face up to his. 'But why didn't you tell me?' All those years of misery for nothing.

His mouth quirked wryly. 'I was terrified of your reaction if you knew just how I felt.' He kissed her lightly on the tip of her freckled nose. 'I knew you were attracted to me—'

'You conceited wretch,' Tamsin said, grinning.

'But I didn't want to be the object of a fleeting physical infatuation and you were still young enough to confuse—'

'Desire with love,' Tamsin broke in softly, remembering his words to her and how she'd misinterpreted them. 'But why did you disappear to America? Without even saying goodbye?'

'I didn't trust myself with you any longer,' he said simply. 'Then when I returned, you froze me out completely, acted as if you could hardly bear to have me in the same room.'

'I was hurt,' she said quietly.

'And besides, you were always with Tom,' he groaned. 'I was so damn jealous.'

Tamsin looked at him incredibly. 'There's only ever been you,' she said softly and gave a blissful sigh as his mouth took possession of hers.

Raising his head, Jordan smiled down into her dazed eyes. 'You do realize that you seem to have overcome your phobia?'

'Yes.' Tamsin smiled back up at him and then became aware that they had an audience.

A young, white-faced woman, holding a bawling toddler in her arms, was hovering by the car. Breaking free from Jordan's arms, Tamsin turned towards her.

'I'm so sorry,' the woman began. 'I don't know what happened. One minute, Tommy was holding on to my hand and then the next moment, he was running into the road.' Her eyes encompassed Jordan. 'Thank God you're not hurt.' Her gaze dropped to the car.

'The insurance will take care of everything,' Jordan assured her swiftly.

'If you hadn't been driving so slowly, reacted so quickly...' She shuddered. 'Thank you,' she said quietly, her hold tightening on the small boy. 'You must be shaken. I live at number twelve. Please come and have a cup of tea...use the phone.'

'Thank you,' Jordan murmured courteously. 'But my fiancée lives just across the road.'

'Oh, I see. Well, if you're sure you're all right...' Hesitating for a second, she turned and walked away.

Tamsin glanced up at Jordan. 'Fiancée?' she enquired sweetly. 'Aren't you taking a little for granted?' she teased him.

'Oh, no,' he said softly. 'That's one thing I shall never do, Tamsin. Take you for granted.'

'Oh, Tamsin darling, that is the best wedding present you could have given me!' Anne Keston exclaimed with delight. 'I didn't think anything could make today more perfect—' unconsciously, she glanced down at the shining gold band on her left hand '—but you just have!'

Her mouth curving in that idiotic smile that seemed to have become a permanent fixture of late, Tamsin returned her mother's hug.

'Andrew and I were wondering when you and Jordan would come to your senses!'

Tamsin's grin widened as she smoothed down the skirt of her silky blue bridesmaid's dress. She couldn't remember ever seeing her mother look so happy or so serenely beautiful. The day *had* been perfect, from the simple, moving ceremony in the local church to the reception for family and close friends back at Swallow Lodge.

'I think I've got everything.' Slipping on the soft peach jacket over her matching dress, her mother glanced swiftly round the room before closing her small overnight case. The rest of her luggage had already been stowed in the back of the limousine that would shortly be taking her and Andrew to London, where they would spend the first night of their honeymoon in a luxurious hotel, before flying out to the Greek Islands the following day. 'By the way, darling, did I ever thank you for falling off your bike?'

'No, you didn't, actually,' Tamsin admonished straight-faced, her thoughts immediately flying back over the years to that miraculous afternoon that had brought both Andrew and Jordan into their lives.

'Oh, heavens, I'm going to be a grandmother and I feel about eighteen!'

Mother's and daughter's eyes met and they both began to giggle like teenagers, sobering up at the light tap on the door, which opened to admit Andrew.

'Jordan is the second luckiest man in the world,' he said simply, kissing Tamsin on the cheek.

Her gaze instantly darted to the tall, lean figure behind him, the expression in the blue eyes making her dizzy. No, she was the lucky one, the luckiest, happiest person alive.

She started to follow her mother and Andrew down the landing when Jordan shot out a hand to restrain her, pushing her gently back into the room.

'Jordan, they're just about to leave. . . .' she protested weakly as his mouth came down on hers.

'I'm just following tradition,' he informed her solemnly as he raised his head.

'Tradition?' she echoed, curling her arms around his neck, loving him so much that it hurt as she looked into the brilliant eyes.

'The bridesmaid and the best man. . .' He paused to give her another long, lingering kiss.

'Now, now, you two. . .'

Simultaneously, they looked round and saw Mrs. Duncan standing in the open doorway, an expression of mock disapproval on her face.

'You've the rest of your lives for this, so just behave yourselves for five minutes and go down and see your parents off!'

'Yes, Mrs. Duncan,' Jordan said meekly and catching the plump woman off guard swept her up in a huge bear-hug.

Tamsin burst into laughter. *The rest of your lives . . .*

UNLOCK THE DOOR TO GREAT ROMANCE AT BRIDE'S BAY RESORT

Join Harlequin's new across-the-lines series, set in an exclusive hotel on an island off the coast of South Carolina.

Seven of your favorite authors will bring you exciting stories about fascinating heroes and heroines discovering love at Bride's Bay Resort.

Look for these fabulous stories coming to a store near you beginning in January 1996.

Harlequin American Romance #613 in January
Matchmaking Baby by Cathy Gillen Thacker

Harlequin Presents #1794 in February
Indiscretions by Robyn Donald

Harlequin Intrigue #362 in March
Love and Lies by Dawn Stewardson

Harlequin Romance #3404 in April
Make Believe Engagement by Day Leclaire

Harlequin Temptation #588 in May
Stranger in the Night by Roseanne Williams

Harlequin Superromance #695 in June
Married to a Stranger by Connie Bennett

Harlequin Historicals #324 in July
Dulcie's Gift by Ruth Langan

Visit Bride's Bay Resort each month wherever Harlequin books are sold.

HARLEQUIN ®

BBAYG

Take 4 bestselling love stories FREE

Plus get a FREE surprise gift!

Special Limited-time Offer

Mail to Harlequin Reader Service®

   3010 Walden Avenue
   P.O. Box 1867
   Buffalo, N.Y. 14240-1867

YES! Please send me 4 free Harlequin Romance® novels and my free surprise gift. Then send me 6 brand-new novels every month, which I will receive months before they appear in bookstores. Bill me at the low price of $2.67 each plus 25¢ delivery and applicable sales tax if any*. That's the complete price and a savings of over 10% off the cover prices—quite a bargain! I understand that accepting the books and gift places me under no obligation ever to buy any books. I can always return a shipment and cancel at any time. Even if I never buy another book from Harlequin, the 4 free books and the surprise gift are mine to keep forever.

116 BPA A3UK

Name	(PLEASE PRINT)	
Address	Apt. No.	
City	State	Zip

This offer is limited to one order per household and not valid to present Harlequin Romance® subscribers. *Terms and prices are subject to change without notice. Sales tax applicable in N.Y.

UROM-698   ©1990 Harlequin Enterprises Limited

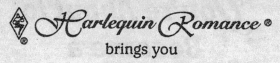

Harlequin Romance ®

brings you

How the West Was Wooed!

We've rounded up twelve of our most popular authors, and the result is a whole year of romance, Western style. Every month we'll be bringing you a spirited, independent woman whose heart is about to be lassoed by a rugged, handsome, one-hundred-percent cowboy! Watch for...

- July: A RANCH, A RING AND EVERYTHING—Val Daniels

- August: TEMPORARY TEXAN—Heather Allison

- September: SOMETHING OLD, SOMETHING NEW—
  Catherine Leigh

- October: WYOMING WEDDING—Barbara McMahon

Available wherever Harlequin books are sold.

HITCH-6

You're About to Become a
Privileged
Woman

**Reap the rewards of fabulous free gifts and
benefits with proofs-of-purchase from
Harlequin and Silhouette books**

Pages & Privileges™

It's our way of thanking you for
buying our books at your
favorite retail stores.

✂

**PROOF OF
PURCHASE**
HR-PP142

Offer expires October 31, 1996

**Harlequin and Silhouette—
the most privileged readers in the world!**

For more information about Harlequin and
Silhouette's PAGES & PRIVILEGES program call the
Pages & Privileges Benefits Desk: 1-503-794-2499

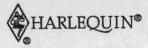

HARLEQUIN®